Dear Reader,

When my editor first approached me about doing a Sleeping Beauty theme for my next book, I was so excited. I adore classic fairy tales! I enjoyed the challenge of incorporating some of the essential elements of the Brothers Grimm fairy tale while doing my own spin on it. No pun intended! Alas, there are no spindles in my story, but I did make my heroine, Artemisia, a talented embroiderer living in an ancient ivy-clad castle. And of course, my hero, Luca Ferrantelli, is the dashingly handsome prince who awakens her with a kiss.

In the Brothers Grimm fairy tale, Sleeping Beauty is asleep for one hundred years in a glass coffin due to a curse put upon her as a child. Artie, in my story, suffers from severe social anxiety and hasn't left the *castello* for a decade. She is psychologically asleep to her potential, and it is only when she meets Luca that she is able to gradually break free of the curse of guilt that has contained her since she was a teenager.

Something rather spooky happened as I was writing this story. I suddenly realized I didn't just have one Sleeping Beauty in my novel—I had three! Luca was also a Sleeping Beauty and so, too, was Artie's friend and housekeeper at the *castello*, Rosa.

Social anxiety is a crippling condition and is notoriously difficult to overcome, but it can be done. Some people very close to me have suffered from it, and their courage in trying to overcome it has always inspired and impressed me.

Best wishes,

Melanie XX

Once Upon a Temptation

Will they live passionately ever after?

Once upon a time, in a land far, far away, there was a billionaire—or eight! Each billionaire had riches beyond your wildest imagination. Still, they were each missing something: love. But the path to true love is never easy...even if you're one of the world's richest men!

Inspired by fairy tales like *Beauty and the Beast* and *Little Red Riding Hood*, the Once Upon a Temptation collection will take you on a passion-filled journey of ultimate escapism.

Fall in love with...

Cinderella's Royal Secret by Lynne Graham

Beauty and Her One-Night Baby by Dani Collins

Shy Queen in the Royal Spotlight
by Natalie Anderson

Claimed in the Italian's Castle by Caitlin Crews

Expecting His Billion-Dollar Scandal
by Cathy Williams

Taming the Big Bad Billionaire by Pippa Roscoe

The Flaw in His Marriage Plan by Tara Pammi

His Innocent's Passionate Awakening
by Melanie Milburne

Melanie Milburne

HIS INNOCENT'S
PASSIONATE AWAKENING

PRESENTS

Recycling programs
for this product may
not exist in your area.

ISBN-13: 978-1-335-89379-6

His Innocent's Passionate Awakening

Copyright © 2020 by Melanie Milburne

Harlequin Enterprises ULC
22 Adelaide St. West, 40th Floor
Toronto, Ontario M5H 4E3, Canada
www.Harlequin.com

Printed in U.S.A.

Melanie Milburne read her first Harlequin novel at the age of seventeen, in between studying for her final exams. After completing a master's degree in education, she decided to write a novel, and thus her career as a romance author was born. Melanie is an ambassador for the Australian Childhood Foundation and a keen dog lover and trainer. She enjoys long walks in the Tasmanian bush. In 2015 Melanie won the HOLT Medallion, a prestigious award honoring outstanding literary talent.

Books by Melanie Milburne

Harlequin Presents

The Tycoon's Marriage Deal
A Virgin for a Vow
Blackmailed into the Marriage Bed
Tycoon's Forbidden Cinderella
The Return of Her Billionaire Husband

Conveniently Wed!

Bound by a One-Night Vow
Penniless Virgin to Sicilian's Bride
Billionaire's Wife on Paper

Secret Heirs of Billionaires

Cinderella's Scandalous Secret

The Scandal Before the Wedding

Claimed for the Billionaire's Convenience
The Venetian One-Night Baby

Visit the Author Profile page
at Harlequin.com for more titles.

Dedicated to Rachel Bailey—a fellow dog lover, romance writer and awesome brainstorming partner! Thanks for being such a wonderful friend xxxxx. Licks and cuddles from Polly and Lily, too.

CHAPTER ONE

Artemisia Bellante stared at her father's lawyer in abject horror. 'But there must be some mistake. How can Castello Mireille be…be *mortgaged?* It's been in my father's family for generations. Papa never mentioned anything about owing money to a bank.'

'He didn't owe it to a bank.' The lawyer, Bruno Rossi, pushed a sheaf of papers across the desk towards Artie, his expression grave. 'Have you heard of Luca Ferrantelli? He runs his late father's global property developing company. He's also a wine and olive producer with a keen interest in rare grape varieties, some of which are on the Castello Mireille estate.'

Artie lowered her gaze to the papers in front of her, a light shiver racing down her spine like a stray current of electricity. 'I've vaguely heard of him…' She might have spent years living in isolation on her family's ancient estate but even she had heard of the handsome billionaire playboy. And seen pictures. And swooned just like any other woman between the ages of fifteen and fifty.

She raised her gaze back to the lawyer's. 'But how did this happen? I know Papa had to let some of the gardeners go to keep costs down and insisted we cut back on housekeeping expenses, but he didn't mention anything about borrowing money from anyone. I don't understand how Signor Ferrantelli now owns most, if not all, my family's home. Why didn't Papa tell me before he died?'

To find out like this was beyond embarrassing. And deeply hurtful. Was this her father's way of forcing his shut-in daughter out of the nest by pushing her to the verge of bankruptcy?

Where would she find the sort of money to dig herself out of this catastrophic mess?

Bruno shifted his glasses further up the bridge of his Roman nose. 'Apparently your father and Luca's father had some sort of business connection in the past. He contacted Luca for financial help when the storm damage hit the *castello* late last year. His insurance policy had lapsed and he knew he would have no choice but to sell if someone didn't bail him out.'

Artie rapid-blinked. 'The insurance lapsed? But why didn't he tell me? I'm his only child. The only family he had left. Surely he should have trusted me enough to tell me the truth about our finances.'

Bruno Rossi made a shrugging movement with one shoulder. 'Pride. Embarrassment. Shame. The usual suspects in cases like this. He had to mortgage the estate to pay for the repairs. Luca Ferrantelli seemed the best option—the only option, considering your father's poor state of health. But the repayment plan didn't go according to schedule, which leaves you in an awkward position.'

Artie wrinkled her brow, a tension headache stabbing at the backs of her eyes like scorching hot needles. Was this a nightmare? Would she suddenly wake up and find this was nothing but a terrifying dream?

Please let this not be real.

'Surely Papa knew he would have to eventually pay back the money he borrowed from Signor Ferrantelli? How could he have let it get to this? And wouldn't Luca Ferrantelli have done due diligence and realised Papa wouldn't be able to pay it back? Or was that

Ferrantelli's intention all along—to take the *castello* off us?'

Bruno leaned forward in his chair with a sigh. 'Your father was a good man, Artie, but he wasn't good at managing finances, especially since the accident. There have been a lot of expenses, as you know, with running the estate since he came home from hospital. Your mother was the one with the financial clout to keep things in the black, but of course, after she died in the accident, it naturally fell to him. Unfortunately, he didn't always listen to advice from his accountants and financial advisors.'

He gave a rueful movement of his lips and continued.

'I'm sure I wouldn't be the first person to tell you how much the accident changed him. He fired his last three accountants because they told him things had to change. Luca Ferrantelli's offer of financial help has meant you could nurse your father here until he passed away, but now of course, unless you can find the money to pay off the mortgage, it will remain in Luca's possession.'

Over her dead body, it would. No way was she handing over her family's home without a fight, even if it would be a David and Goliath mismatch. Artie would find some way of winning.

She *had* to.

Artie did her best to ignore the beads of sweat forming between her shoulder blades. The drumbeat of panic in her chest. The hammering needles behind her eyeballs. The sense of the floor beneath her feet pitching like a paper boat riding a tsunami. 'When and where did Papa meet with Signor Ferrantelli? I've been Papa's full-time carer for the last ten years and don't recall Signor Ferrantelli ever coming here to see him.'

'Maybe he came one day while you were out.'

Out? Artie didn't go *out*.

She wasn't like other people, who could walk out of their homes and meet up with friends. It was impossible for her to be around more than one or two people at a time. Three was very definitely a crowd.

'Maybe...' Artie looked down at the papers again, conscious of warmth filling her cheeks. Her social anxiety was far more effective than a maximum-security prison. She hadn't been outside the *castello* walls since she was fifteen.

Ten years.

A decade.

Two fifths of her life.

As far as she knew, it wasn't common knowledge that she suffered from social anxiety. Her father's dependence on her had made it easy to disguise her fear of crowds. She had relished the role of looking after him. It had given her life a purpose, a focus. She had mostly avoided meeting people when they came to the *castello* to visit her father. She stayed in the background until they left. But barely anyone but her father's doctor and physical therapists had come during the last year or two of his life. Compassion fatigue had worn out his so-called friends. And now that the money had run dry, she could see why they had drifted away, one by one. There wasn't anyone she could turn to. Having been home schooled since her mid-teens, she had lost contact with her school friends. Friends wanted you to socialise with them and that she could never do, so they, too, had drifted away.

She had no friends of her own other than Rosa, the housekeeper.

Artie took a deep breath and blinked to clear her clouded vision. The words in front of her confirmed her worst fears. Her home was mortgaged to the hilt. There was no way a bank would lend her enough funds to get the *castello* out of Luca Ferrantelli's hands. The only job she had ever had was as her father's carer. From fifteen to twenty-five she had taken care of his every need. She had no formal qualifications, no skills other than her embroidery hobby.

She swallowed and pushed the papers back across the desk. 'What about my mother's trust fund? Isn't there enough left for me to pay off the mortgage?'

'There's enough for you to live on for the short-term but not enough to cover the money owed.'

Artie's heart began to beat like a wounded frog. 'How long have I got?' It sounded like a terminal diagnosis, which in some ways it was. She couldn't imagine her life without Castello Mireille. It was her home. Her base. Her anchor.

Her entire world.

Bruno Rossi shuffled the papers back into a neat pile. 'A year or two. But even if you were by some chance to raise finance to keep the estate, the place needs considerable maintenance. Costly maintenance. The storm damage last year showed how vulnerable the *castello* is. The north wing's roof still needs some work, not to mention the conservatory. It will cost millions of euros to—'

'Yes, yes, I know.' Artie pushed back her chair and smoothed her damp palms down her thighs. The *castello* was crumbling around her—she saw evidence of it every single day. But moving out of her home was unthinkable. Impossible.

She literally *couldn't* do it.

Panic tiptoed over her skin like thousands of tiny ants wearing stilettoes. Pressure built in her chest—a crushing weight pushing against her lungs so she couldn't take another breath. She wrapped her arms around her middle, fighting to hold off a full-blown panic attack. She hadn't had one for a while but the threat was always lurking in the murky shadows of her consciousness. It had followed her like a malevolent ghost ever since she came home from hospital from the accident that killed her mother and left her father in a wheelchair.

An accident that wouldn't have occurred if it hadn't been for *her*.

The lawyer cleared his throat. 'There's something else…' The formal quality of his tone changed and another shiver skittered down Artie's spine.

She straightened her shoulders and cupped her elbows with her hands, hoping for a cool and dignified stance but falling way too short. 'W-what?'

'Signor Ferrantelli has proposed a plan for you to repay him. If you fulfil his terms, you will regain full ownership of the *castello* within six months.'

Artie's eyebrows shot up along with her heart rate. And her anxiety grew razorblade wings and flapped frantically against her stomach lining like frenzied bats. How could she ever repay those mortgage payments in such a short space of time? What on earth did he require her to do? 'A plan? What sort of plan?' Her voice came out high and strained like an overused squeaky toy.

'He didn't authorise me to discuss it with you. He insists on speaking to you in person first.' Bruno pushed back his chair, further demonstrating his unwillingness to reveal anything else. 'Signor Ferrantelli has requested a meeting with you in his Milan office nine a.m. sharp, on Monday, to discuss your options.'

Options? What possible options could there

be? None she wanted to think about in any detail. Ice-cold dread slithered into her belly. What nefarious motives could Luca Ferrantelli have towards her? A woman he had never met? And what was with his drill sergeant commands?

Nine a.m. Sharp. In his office. In Milan.

Luca Ferrantelli sounded like a man who issued orders and expected them to be obeyed without question. But there was no way she could go to Milan. Not on Monday. Not any day. She couldn't get as far as the front gate without triggering crippling, stomach-emptying, mind-scattering panic.

Artie released her arms from around her body and gripped the back of the nearest chair. Her heart was racing like it was preparing for the Olympics. 'Tell him to meet me here. It's not convenient for me to go to Milan. I don't drive and, from what you've just told me, I can't afford a taxi or even an Uber.'

'Signor Ferrantelli is a busy man. He expressly told me to tell you he—'

Artie stiffened her spine and raised her chin and ground her teeth behind her cool smile. 'Tell him to meet me here, nine a.m. sharp, on Monday. Or not meet with me at all.'

* * *

Luca Ferrantelli drove his Maserati through the rusty entrance gates of Castello Mireille on Monday morning. The *castello* was like something out of a Grimm brothers' fairy tale. The centuries-old ivy-clad stone building was surrounded by gardens that looked like they hadn't been tended for years, with overgrown hedges, unpruned roses, weed-covered pathways and ancient trees that stood like gnarly sentries. The *castello* had loads of potential—years of running his late father's property development company had taught him how to spot a diamond in the rough.

And speaking of diamonds...

He glanced at the velvet box on the seat next to him containing his late grandmother's engagement ring, and inwardly smiled. Artemisia Bellante would make the perfect temporary bride. Her father, Franco, had emailed Luca a photo of his daughter shortly before he died, asking Luca to make sure she was looked after once he was gone. The photo had planted a seed in Luca's mind—a seed that had taken root and sprouted and blossomed until all he could think about was meeting her—to offer her a way out of her present circumstances. Young, innocent, sheltered—

she was exactly the sort of young woman his conservative grandfather would deem suitable as a Ferrantelli bride.

Time was rapidly running out on convincing his grandfather to accept the chemo he so desperately needed. Luca had a small window of opportunity to get Nonno to change his mind. Luca would do anything—even marry a poverty-stricken heiress—to make sure his elderly and frail *nonno* could live a few more precious years. After all, it was his fault his grandfather had lost the will to live. Didn't he owe Nonno some measure of comfort, given how Luca had torn apart the Ferrantelli family?

A vision of Luca's father, Flavio, and older brother, Angelo, drifted into his mind. Their lifeless bodies pulled from the surf due to his reckless behaviour as a teenager. His reckless behaviour and their love for him—a lethal, deadly combination. Two lives cut short because of him. Two lives and their potential wasted, and his mother and grandparents' happiness permanently, irrevocably destroyed. No one had been the same since that terrible day. No one.

Luca blinked to clear away the vision and gripped the steering wheel with white-knuckled force. He couldn't bring his father and brother back. He couldn't undo the damage he had caused to his mother and Nonna and Nonno. His grandmother had died a year ago and since then, his grandfather had lost the will to live. Nonno was refusing treatment for his very treatable cancer, and if he didn't receive chemotherapy soon he would die. So far, no amount of talking, lecturing, cajoling or bribing or begging on Luca's part had helped changed his grandfather's mind.

But Luca had a plan and he intended to carry it out no matter what. He would bring home a fresh-faced young bride to give hope to his grandfather that the Ferrantelli family line would continue well into the future.

Even if that was nothing but a fairy tale.

Artie watched Luca Ferrantelli's showroom-perfect deep blue Maserati come through the *castello* gates like a prowling lion. The low purr of the engine was audible even here in the formal sitting room. The car's tinted windows made it impossible for her to get a proper glimpse of his face, but the car's sleek profile and throaty growls seemed like a representation of his forthright personality.

Didn't they say a person's choice of car told you a lot about them?

Artie already knew as much as she wanted to know. *More* than she wanted to know. That would teach her for spending the weekend trawling over the internet for any mention of him. Her research had revealed him as a flagrant playboy who brokered property deals and broke female hearts all over the globe. Barely a week went past without a gossip page featuring Luca Ferrantelli with a star-struck sylph-like blonde draped on his arm.

The powerful sports car came to a halt at the front of the *castello*. Artie sucked in a breath as the driver's door opened, her heart giving a sudden kick, her eyes widening as a vision of potent, athletic maleness unfolded from behind the wheel. The internet photos hadn't done him justice. How could it be possible to be so spectacularly attractive? Her pulse fluttered as if someone had injected her veins with thousands of butterflies.

The good-looks fairy godmother had certainly excelled herself when it came to Luca Ferrantelli. Six foot four, lean and athletic, with wavy black hair that was casually styled in a just-out-of-bed or just-combed-with-his-fingers manner, he was the epitome of heart-stopping handsome. Even though she was looking at him from a distance, Artie's heart was stopping and starting like a spluttering engine. How was she going to be when he was in the same room as her? Breathing the same air? Within touching distance?

As if Luca Ferrantelli sensed her gaze on him, he took off his aviator-style sunglasses and locked gazes with her. Something sprang open in her chest and she suddenly couldn't breathe. She quickly stepped away from the window and leaned back against the adjacent wall, clutching a hand to her pulsing throat, heat pouring into her cheeks. She had to get a grip. And fast. The last thing she wanted to do was appear gauche and unsophisticated, but, given she had been out of society for so long, she was at a distinct disadvantage. He was the poster boy for living in the fast lane. She was a wallflower who hadn't been seen in public for a decade.

It was some minutes before the house-keeper, Rosa, led Luca Ferrantelli to where Artie was waiting to receive him, but even so, her pulse was still leaping when the sitting room door opened. What if she became tongue-tied? What if she blushed? What if she broke out in a sweat and couldn't breathe? What if—?

'Signor Ferrantelli to see you,' Rosa announced with a formal nod in Luca's direction, before going out of the room and closing the door behind her with a click.

The first thing Artie noticed was his hair wasn't completely black. There were several strands of steel-grey sprinkled around his temples, which gave him a distinguished, wise-beyond-his-years air. His eyes were framed by prominent eyebrows and were an unusual hazel—a mix of brown and green flecks, fringed by thick, ink-black lashes. His amazing eyes were a kaleidoscope of colours one would normally find in a deeply shadowed forest. His jaw was cleanly shaven but the faint shadow of regrowth around his nose and mouth hinted at the potent male hormones working vigorously behind the scenes.

The atmosphere of the room changed with his presence, as if every stick of furniture, every fibre of carpet and curtains, every portrait frame and the faces of her ancestors contained within them took a collective breath. Stunned by his looks, his commanding presence, his take-charge energy.

'*Buongiorno*, Signorina Bellante.' Luca

Ferrante's voice was like the sound of his car—low and deep, with a sexy rumble that did something strange to the base of her spine. So, too, did seeing his lips move when shaping and pronouncing her name. His lower lip was full and sensual, the top lip only marginally less so, and he had a well-defined philtrum ridge beneath his nose and a shallow cleft in his chin.

Artie slipped her hand into his outstretched one and a zap of electricity shot from her fingers to her core like a lightning bolt. His grip was strong and yet strangely gentle, his fingers long and tanned with a light dusting of dark masculine hair that ran over the backs of his hands and disappeared beneath the cuffs of his business shirt and jacket. Armani, at a guess. And his aftershave an equally intoxicating blend of citrus and spice and sophistication that teased her senses into a stupor.

'*Buongiorno*, Signor Ferrantelli.'

Artie aimed for cool politeness but sounded more like a star-struck teen in front of a Hollywood celebrity. She could feel warm colour blooming in her cheeks. Could feel her heart thumping like it was having some sort of medical crisis. Could feel her female hormones responding to his male ones with little tingles and pulses deep within her body.

Let go of his hand!

Her brain gave the command but her hand was trapped in some kind of weird stasis. It was as if her hand had a mind of its own and was enjoying being held by his warm, dry one, thank you very much. Enjoying it so much, she could feel every whorl of his skin as if it were being engraved, branded into hers.

Luca removed his hand from hers but his gaze kept hers tethered. She couldn't look away if she tried. Magnetic. Enthralling. Mesmerising. His eyes seemed to draw secrets from within her while concealing his own.

'Firstly, allow me to offer my condolences on the recent passing of your father.'

'Grazie.'

She stepped back and waved her still-tingling hand in the direction of the sofa. 'Would you like to sit down? I'll call Rosa to bring in coffee. How do you take it?'

'Black and strong.'

Of course you do.

Artie pressed the intercom pad and summoned Rosa, surreptitiously eyeing him while she requested coffee from the housekeeper.

Everything about Luca Ferrantelli was strong. Strong, determined jaw. Strong, intelligent eyes. A strong and muscled body that hinted at a man who wasn't afraid of pushing himself to the limits of endurance. A man who set goals and didn't let anyone or anything stop him from achieving them.

Artie ended the intercom conversation with Rosa and sat on the nearest sofa, and only then did Luca take the seat opposite. He laid one arm along the back of the sofa in a casually relaxed pose she privately envied. She had to place her hands on the tops of her thighs to stop her knees from trembling. Not from fear but from a strange sense of fizzing excitement. She tried not to stare at his powerfully muscled thighs, his well-formed biceps, the flat plane of his stomach, but her gaze kept drifting over him of its own volition. Drinking in the planes and contours of his face, wondering what was going on behind the screen of his gaze, wondering if his firm lips would soften when he kissed…

Artie blinked and sat up straighter on the sofa, crossing her legs to try and control the wayward urges going on in her lower body. What was wrong with her? He had barely exchanged more than half a dozen words with her and she was undressing him with her eyes. She curled her hands into balls on her lap and fixed a smile on her lips. 'So, how was your drive from Milan? I hope it didn't inconvenience you too much to come here?' Who said she couldn't do small talk?

Luca's half-smile and his glittering forest floor eyes made something slip sideways in her stomach. 'It didn't inconvenience me at all. But we both know that was your intention, was it not?'

Artie forced herself to hold his penetrating gaze. 'Signor Ferrantelli, I am not the sort of woman to jump when a man says jump.'

The dark gleam in his eyes intensified and a hot trickle of something liquid spilled deep in her core. 'You may have no choice, given I now own nine tenths of Castello Mireille, unless you can buy me out within the next twenty-four hours.' There was a don't-mess-with-me warning in his tone that made her want to mess with him to see what would happen.

Artie disguised a swallow, her heart picking up its pace. 'My father's lawyer informed me of the unusual financial arrangement you made with my father. One wonders why you didn't buy all of it off him while you had the chance.'

His gaze was unwavering. 'He was a dying man who deserved some dignity in the last months of his life.'

Artie gave a cynical smile while her blood boiled in her veins and roaring anger bubbled in her chest. 'Do you expect me to believe you felt some measure of compassion for him? Even while you were systematically taking his home away from him ancient stone by ancient stone?'

Luca didn't change his casual posture on the sofa but a ripple of tension passed across his features, tightening his jaw, flaring his nose, hardening his eyes. 'Your father approached me late last year for help. I gave it to him. It was a straightforward business deal. And now I have come to collect on my investment.'

Artie shot up from the sofa as if someone had pressed an ejector switch. She glared at him with the full force of her fury, chest heaving like she had just completed a marathon without training first. 'You can't take my home off me. I won't allow it.'

Luca Ferrantelli's gaze was diamond-hard.

'My intention is to give the *castello* back to you—after a time. And for a price.'

Something heavy landed on the floor of her belly. 'What price? You must know I can't possibly raise the necessary funds to pay out the mortgage?'

He held her gaze in a lock that made the backs of her knees tingle. 'I will erase the debt and give the deeds of the *castello* back if you agree to be my wife for six months.'

CHAPTER TWO

ARTIE STARED AT HIM in open-mouthed shock, her heart pounding like it was going to punch its way out of her chest. Had she heard him correctly? Was her imagination playing tricks on her? Putting words in his mouth he couldn't possibly have said? Had he said *wife?* W.I.F.E? The woman a man chose to spend the rest of his life with in a contract of love and commitment?

'Your…*what?*'

He hooked one ankle over his bent knee, his finger idly flicking the zipper toggle on his Italian leather boot. *Flick. Flick. Flick.* So relaxed. So casual. So confident and in control it was maddening.

'You heard—I need a wife for six months. On paper.' The note of self-assurance in his voice made her dislike of him go up another notch.

On paper? Her eyes widened while her feminine ego shrank. She might not be a social butterfly or model material, but as far as she knew she hadn't broken any mirrors lately. 'You mean a marriage of convenience?'

'But of course.'

Why 'but of course'? It was ridiculous to be affronted by his unusual proposal, but what woman wanted to be dismissed outright as a potential lover?

But why would he want you? the voice of her conscience sneered. *Who would want you? You killed your mother, you maimed your father—all for the sake of going to a stupid party.*

Rosa, the housekeeper, came in at that moment carrying a tray with cups and saucers and a steaming percolator of freshly brewed coffee. Rosa handed Luca a cup before turning to give one to Artie. But as soon as Rosa left the room Artie put her coffee on a side table, not trusting her shaking hands to bring the cup safely to her tombstone-dry mouth. Her conscience was right. Why would he want to marry *her?* Why would anyone?

Luca lowered his crossed ankle to the floor and, reaching for his cup, took a sip of his coffee as if this was a regular old coffee morning. Not one in which he had delivered a bombshell proposal to a virtual stranger.

'May I ask, why me?' Artie inserted into the silence. 'You surely have no shortage of far more suitable candidates for the role.' Socialites. Supermodels. Not a shut-in like her.

Luca put his cup back in its saucer with unnerving and methodical precision. It hinted at the man he was—self-assured, focused, confident he could get anything he set his mind to. 'Your father was the one who planted the idea in my—'

'My *father?*' Artie choked over the words.

'He was concerned about your future, given how badly his financial situation had become and how it would impact on you long-term. He wanted you well provided for, so I devised a plan to make sure we both got what we wanted. You get to keep the *castello*. I get a temporary wife.'

Artie clasped her hands together, trying to keep control of her galloping pulse. Her legs were threatening to give way beneath her but she was reluctant to sit back down, because it would bring her closer to him than she wanted to be. 'But why would you want me to be your…your wife?' Saying the word felt strange on her lips and yet her mind ran with the image it evoked. Images popped into her head of her wearing a white dress and standing next to Luca at an altar. His arms going around her, drawing him closer to his muscled body. His mouth slowly coming down to seal hers in a kiss…

'You're exactly the sort of woman my grandfather would approve of as my bride,' Luca said, his gaze drifting to her mouth as if he was having the same thoughts as her. About kissing, touching, needing, wanting.

Artie arched her eyebrows. 'Oh, really? Why is that?'

His lips curved in a satirical smile. 'You're the sweet, homespun type—or so your father led me to believe.'

What else had her father told him about her? She had made him promise not to tell anyone about her social anxiety. Had he broken that promise? She was pretty sure he hadn't told Bruno Rossi, the lawyer, otherwise he would have mentioned it yesterday. It was her shameful little secret. Her father's dependence on her since the accident had made it easy for her to hide it from others, but with him no longer here…

Artie kept her expression neutral but on the inside, she was seething. How dared her father set her up for auction to this incorrigible man? It was positively feudal. And why did Luca Ferrantelli want to please his grandfather? What was at stake if he didn't? 'Look, Signor Ferrantelli, I think there's been some sort of misunderstanding between you and my father. I can't think of a single set of circumstances in which I would ever consider marrying you.'

Luca's mocking smile broadened. 'Perhaps not as sweet and biddable as your father said.' His tone was musing, the lazy sweep of his gaze assessing. 'But, no matter. You will do.'

She straightened her shoulders and sent him a look so frosty icicles could have formed on her eyelashes. 'Please leave. We have nothing left to discuss.'

Luca remained seated on the sofa, still in that annoyingly relaxed pose. But his eyes contained a glint of intractability that made her wonder if she was wise to lock horns with him. She had no experience in dealing with powerful men. She had no experience, period. Any fight between them would be like Tinkerbell trying to take down a Titan.

'The way I see it, you don't have any choice. You will lose the *castello* if you don't agree to marry me.'

Artie ground her teeth and clenched her fists, anger flicking along her nerve endings like a power surge of electricity. It was all she could do not to slap him. She pictured herself doing it—landing her palm against his lean and chiselled jaw with a resounding slap. Imagining how his rougher skin would feel under the soft skin of her palm. Imagining how he might grasp her by the wrist and haul her closer and slam his mouth down on hers in a passionate kiss…

Eek! She shouldn't have watched *Gone with the Wind* so many times.

She stretched out one arm and pointed her index finger towards the door. 'Get. Out.'

Luca raised his long, lean, athletic frame from the sofa with leonine grace and came to stand in front of her. She fought not to step back, determined to show he didn't intimidate her with his commanding, disturbing presence. Even though he did. Big time. She had to crane her neck to maintain eye-contact, and give her traitorous body a stern talking-to for reacting to his closeness with a hitch of her breath and an excited leap of her pulse.

'I'll give you twenty-four hours to consider my proposal.'

Artie raised her chin to a defiant height.

'I've already considered it and flatly turned it down. I'll give you the same answer tomorrow, so don't waste your time or mine by coming back.'

His lazy smile ignited a light behind his eyes as if her refusal had thrilled rather than disappointed him. 'You have a lot to lose, Signorina Bellante.' He swung his gaze around the room before bringing it back to meet hers. 'Are you sure you want to throw all this away for the sake of your pride?'

'Pride has nothing to do with my decision. If and when I marry, it will be for love.'

The loud cackling of her conscience rang in Artie's ears like clanging bells.

Marry for love? You? Who's going to love you?

His eyes flicked to her mouth and lingered there for a heart-stopping moment. 'You love this place, do you not? Your family's home for how many centuries? If that's not marrying for love, I don't know what is.' The deep, mellifluous tone of his voice had a mesmerising effect on her. She had to fight to stay focused on resisting him. It would be so easy to say yes. To have all her problems solved by agreeing to his plan—even if by doing so it threw up new ones. Dangerous ones. Exciting ones.

Artie pressed her lips together. 'Of course I love it. It's the only home I've ever known.'

The only home I can ever know.

His eyes meshed with hers. Dark, mysterious, unknowable. 'If you don't marry me, you will lose it. And I won't lose a wink of sleep about taking it off you. Business is business. I don't let emotions cloud the issue. Think about it, hmm?'

She tried to ignore the cynical gleam in his eyes. Tried to ignore the slippery eels of panic writhing in her belly. Tried not to think about her home being lost for ever. Of it being made into a plush hotel with strangers walking through every room, occupying every private space, every special corner made into a flashy showpiece instead of a private sanctuary where her most precious memories were housed. 'You can't force me out of my home. I have some rights, surely?'

'Your father signed those over to me when he begged for my help.'

Artie raised her chin, summoning every bit of willpower she possessed to stand up to his monumental ego. 'You came here expecting me to say yes, didn't you? Does anyone ever say no to you?'

'Not often.' He reached inside his jacket pocket and took a velvet box and held it out to her in the middle of his palm. 'This might help you come to a decision.'

Artie reared back from the box like it was a cockroach. 'You think you can bribe me with diamonds?'

'Not just diamonds.' He flicked open the velvet box with his thumb and a glittering sapphire and diamond engagement ring winked at her. 'Take it. Try it on for size.'

Artie brought her gaze back to his, her mouth tightly compressed. 'No, thank you.'

There was a beat or two of silence.

Luca snapped the lid of the ring box closed and placed it on the coffee table. If she had offended him with her point-blank refusal then he didn't show it in his expression.

'I'll be back for your decision tomorrow. *Ciao*.'

He gave a mock bow, and without another word he walked out of the salon, closing the door on his exit.

Artie let out a scalding breath, her body sagging with the aftershocks of too much cortisol racing through her system. She sat back on the sofa before she fell down, her legs shaking, her hands trembling, her mind whirling.

How could this be happening? It was like something out of a period drama. She was being blackmailed into marrying a man she didn't know in order to save her home. What had her father been thinking to plant such a ridiculous idea in Luca Ferrantelli's head? This was nothing but a business deal to Luca but it was her home that was on the line. And not just her home—her security. Her future. She would have nothing to fall back on if she didn't have the *castello*.

It was her heritage.

Her birthright.

Her safety.

How dared Luca Ferrantelli dangle it before her like a plump, juicy carrot in front of a dumb donkey?

She was *not* going to be a pawn in his game. If he thought she was so desperate for a husband she would say yes to the first man who asked her, then he had better think again.

Rosa came back into the salon to collect the coffee cups. 'Your guest left, then. What did he want?' Her eyes went to the ring box on the coffee table. 'Ooh, what's this?'

Artie got up from the sofa and speared her fingers through her hair. 'You wouldn't believe me if I told you. *Grr.* I don't know how I stopped myself from slapping him. He's the most detestable man I've ever met.'

Rosa's look was wry. 'Like you've met heaps of men. Just saying…' She prised open the lid of the ring box and whistled through her teeth. '*Mamma mia.* That is what I call an engagement ring.'

Artie snatched the box off her and snapped it shut and clutched it tightly in her hand. 'If he's representative of the men outside the *castello* walls, then I'm glad I haven't met heaps of them. Do you know what he said? He wants to marry me. For six months. A paper marriage or some such nonsense. And do you know what's worse? Papa put the idea in his head. Luca Ferrantelli will only give me back the *castello*, debt-free, if I marry him.'

'And you said?'

Artie frowned. 'What do you think I said? I said an emphatic, don't-ask-me-again *no.*'

Rosa loaded the coffee percolator onto the tray with implacable calm. 'Would you say yes if the marriage wasn't on paper?'

'No, of course not.'

'Then what's the problem? Don't you trust him to keep his word?'

Artie put her hands on her hips. She could feel the ring box digging into the soft skin of her palm but did her best to ignore it. She would *not* look at it again. She would not look at those sparkling diamonds and that impossibly blue sapphire and imagine a life free of financial stress.

She would not think of being Luca Ferrantelli's bride.

She. Would. Not.

'Are you seriously telling me I should accept his crazy proposal? Are you out of your mind?' Artie narrowed her gaze and added, 'Wait—do you know something about this? Did Papa talk to you about his scheme to marry me off to a stranger to settle his debts?'

Rosa picked up the coffee tray and held it in front of her body, her expression set in her customary pragmatic lines. 'Your father was worried about you in the weeks before he died—about what would happen to you once he was gone. You gave up your life for him these last few years. He shouldn't have asked it of you and nor should he have run the estate the way he did, but he was never the same after the accident. But you have a chance now to turn things around. To reclaim your life and your inheritance. And Luca Ferrantelli can't be much of a stranger to your father, otherwise he wouldn't have gone to him for help. Why would he have asked Luca if he didn't trust him to do the right thing by you? Six months isn't long. And as long as everything is legally sound, you've got nothing to lose and everything to gain.'

Artie tossed the ring box on the sofa. 'I can't believe you think I should marry that odious man.'

'You can't stay locked away here for ever, Artie. It's not healthy. Your father desperately wanted you to move on with your—'

Artie blew out a breath of exasperation. 'I *can't* leave. I thought you of all people understood. You've seen me at my worst. I feel paralysed with anxiety as soon as I get to the front gates. It's not as if I want to be like this. I can't help it.'

Nothing had helped. Medication. Home visits by a psychologist. Meditation and mindfulness. Nothing had freed her from the curse of her phobia. She had resigned herself to a lifetime of living in isolation.

What else could she do but accept her lot in life?

Rosa shifted her lips from side to side, her dark brown eyes serious. 'You'll have no choice but to leave if the *castello* is sold out from under you.'

The thought of leaving her home, having it taken it away from her by force, made her skin pepper with goosebumps and her heart pound with dread. She had tried so many times to imagine a life outside of Castello Mireille. But it was like a pipedream that never could be realised. It was completely and utterly out of her reach.

Artie glanced at the ring box on the sofa, her heart giving a funny little hopscotch. 'Luca Ferrantelli is an international playboy. He changes lovers every week. What sort of husband is he going to be?'

'You'll never know if you don't marry him, *sì*?' Rosa said. 'Convince him to marry you here at the *castello*—you won't have to leave at all. It's a marriage in name only so there won't be a honeymoon. In six months, you'll have full ownership again. Plus, a gorgeous ring to keep. Problem solved.'

Eek! She hadn't even thought about a honeymoon. Luca wanted a bride but not *that* sort of bride…or did he? Her lower body tingled at the thought of his hands touching her. His mouth pressing against hers. His body doing things to hers she had only fantasised about and never experienced.

Artie pressed her fingers against her temples once Rosa had left the room. What crazy parallel universe had she stumbled into that even the housekeeper thought she should marry Luca Ferrantelli? She let out a ragged breath and looked around the salon. The black velvet ring box on the white sofa seemed to signify the either/or choice she had to make. The sofa cushions still contained the impression of Luca's tall athletic body. The air still smelt faintly of his citrus and spice aftershave. Her heartrate was still not quite back to normal.

Would it ever be again?

Meeting Luca Ferrantelli had jolted her into an intense awareness of her femininity. Her body felt alive—tinglingly alive in a way it never had before. Her mind might have decided Luca was the most obnoxious man she'd ever met but her body hadn't got the memo. It was operating off script, responding to him in ways she had never thought possible. Every appraising look he cast her way, every smouldering twinkle in his hazel eyes, every lazy smile, had heated her blood and upped her pulse and fried her brain until even *she* was thinking about accepting his proposal.

Artie walked back to the sofa and picked up the ring box. She curled her fingers around it, telling herself she would put it in the safe until Luca came back tomorrow. But suddenly her fingers were prising open the lid. The ring glinted at her as if to say, *Put me on*.

It was the most beautiful ring she had ever seen. She might not be able to window shop like other people but she did plenty of shopping and browsing online. She ran her fingertip over the top of the arabesque setting, stunned by the ring's exquisite design and breathtaking quality. Money was no object to filthy rich men like Luca Ferrantelli. He thought he could dangle a ridiculously expensive diamond in front of her nose and she would accept his stupid proposal without question.

She stared at the ring some more, turning the box this way so she could see how the diamonds picked up the light coming in from the windows. It was probably too big for her anyway. Artie pulled her lower lip inside her mouth. What would it hurt to try it on just the once? No one had to know. She hadn't been in a bricks-and-mortar jewellery shop since she was a teenager, when her mother bought her a pair of earrings. This was her chance to do what others took for granted.

She took the ring out of the box and set the box down on the table again. She slipped the ring on her left ring finger, pushing it past her second knuckle. It was kind of weird that it was a perfect fit. She couldn't stop staring at it. The sheer brilliance of the diamonds and the deep blue of the sapphire stole her breath clean away.

'Don't get too comfortable there,' Artie addressed the ring. 'I'm not keeping you.'

The ring glinted back at her as if to say, *Are you sure about that?*

Artie took off the ring, placed it back in its velvet box and closed the lid with a definitive snap. She held the box in the middle of her palm, glaring at it like it contained a lethal insect. 'I'm not looking at you again, do you hear me?' She left the box on the coffee table and went to where Rosa was working in the kitchen.

Rosa looked up from where she was preparing vegetables for soup. 'Did the ring fit?'

Artie pursed her lips. 'What makes you think I tried it on?'

Rosa gave a knowing smile. 'It's not every

day a girl gets to try on a ring as stunning as that.'

Artie frowned. 'I thought you'd be on my side. Aren't you the least bit concerned about my situation?'

'I'm deeply concerned you're going to lose everything if you don't do what Luca Ferrantelli says,' Rosa said. 'You could do a lot worse than him for a husband. He's handsome and rich and will no doubt spoil you, if that ring is any indication.'

'What if I don't want to be spoilt?'

Rosa picked up an onion and held it in her palm. 'See this? Men like Luca Ferrantelli are like this onion. You're only looking at the surface of him—the façade he shows the world. Peel back the layers and you'll see the man behind the mask. You never know—you might be pleasantly surprised at what you find.'

'And how will I know if peeling back his layers reduces me to tears like that onion will?'

'That's a risk we all take when we get close to someone.' Rosa sliced into the onion with a knife. 'And God knows, you're never going to get close to anyone living on your own here. This is a lifeline and you'd be a fool not to take it.'

Maybe Rosa was right, because, if Artie didn't marry Luca Ferrantelli she would have to leave the *castello*. Permanently.

She couldn't allow that to happen.

No matter what.

But how could she work this to her advantage? What could Luca do for her in return? Apart from buying her a stunningly beautiful engagement ring that just begged to come out of that box and sit proudly on her finger. Artie went back to the salon and picked up the velvet box. She told herself she was going to put it in the safe until Luca returned the following day. But before she could stop herself, she opened the box and took the ring out and placed it back on her finger. She promised herself she would only wear it for a couple of hours, just for the heck of it. Then, once she got tired of it, she would put it back in the box and hand it back to Luca tomorrow with a firm, *Thanks, but no, thanks.*

She couldn't possibly marry him…*could she?*

Later that evening, Artie was doing her embroidery when she suddenly realised the ring wasn't on her finger. She jumped off the sofa and searched around the scatter cushions, her heart racing. Where was it? Had it fallen off somewhere? Oh, God. Oh, God. Oh, God. The ring was worth a fortune. Luca would be furious if she lost his blasted ring. He had no right to buy her such an expensive ring. Her stomach pitched. Would he want her to replace it? Yes, he would.

Rosa came in at that point. 'Look, I know things are bad financially but surely you don't have to search the back of the sofa for loose change?'

Artie swung around to face her, eyes wide in panic. 'I can't find Luca's wretched engagement ring!'

Rosa frowned. 'Didn't you put it in the safe?'

'No, I stupidly put it on for a couple of hours.' Artie tossed all the scatter cushions on the floor and began lifting off the sofa cushions to no avail. 'What am I going to do?'

Rosa joined in the search. 'You'll have to retrace your steps. Where have you been in the last few hours? Did you go outside to the garden?'

'No, I've only been indoors.'

Artie emptied her embroidery basket onto the floor—thimbles, reels of thread, needles going everywhere. The disorder on the floor in front of her was the same as inside her mind. Chaos. Tangled thoughts. Prickling conscience.

'It must be here somewhere. Oh, God, how could I lose it?'

She stuffed the embroidery items haphazardly back in the basket, pricking her finger with one of her needles.

'Ouch.' She stuck her finger in her mouth and sucked up the droplets of blood. She removed her finger from her mouth and gave Rosa a baleful look. 'He had no right to give me such an expensive ring. I'll have to marry him now.'

But deep down you want to, don't you? Marriage to Luca Ferrantelli just might give you some control over your life. The control you've been seeking for a long time. Money. Freedom. Not to mention a wickedly handsome 'paper' husband...

Rosa bent down and carefully sorted through Artie's basket for a moment. 'Ah, here it is.' She handed Artie the engagement ring. 'You'd better put it back on and leave it on until you give it back to Signor Ferrantelli.'

Give it back?

Lose her one chance of taking back control of her life?

Lose her home?

Artie slipped the ring back on her finger, her thoughts finally untangling. 'I'm not giving it back. Maybe you're right. This is my chance—maybe my only chance—to take control of my life. I'm going to make this work for me. On my terms. It's only for six months—what have I got to lose?'

Rosa raised one brow. 'Your heart?'

Artie set her mouth in a determined line. 'Not going to happen. This is a business deal. If Luca Ferrantelli can keep his emotions out of this, then so can I.'

Luca could not remember looking forward to a meeting more than returning to the Castello Mireille the following day to see Artemisia Bellante. Something about her intrigued him in a way few people did. He'd expected her to be biddable and submissive and instead found her spirited defiance a refreshing change from all the sycophants who surrounded him, pandering to his every whim. He'd found it so hard to take his eyes off her—slim, but with generous curves in all the right places, flashing brown eyes, wild, curly dark brown hair and a ski-slope nose, a stubborn chin and a cherry-red mouth—he'd almost offered her a real marriage. Only joking. No real marriages for him. Ever. He neither wanted nor needed love from a partner. Love was a reckless emotion that had the potential to cause immeasurable harm. He'd had a ringside seat to see just how much harm.

But a six-month hands-off arrangement to give his grandfather the motivation to get chemo was definitely doable. He hadn't been able to save his father or brother but he could save his grandfather. And marrying Artemisia Bellante was the way to do it. The only way.

In all their phone and email conversations, Franco Bellante had told him Artemisia was shy around men. Luca hadn't seen too much shyness. He'd seen sass and spirit and a damped down sensuality that was irresistibly attractive. He'd seen her surreptitious glances at his mouth and felt the supercharged energy in the air when their gazes collided. Did that mean she would be interested in tweaking the terms of their paper marriage?

Don't even think about it.

Luca knew how to control his impulses. He had learned the hard way not to rush into things without careful consideration first. Artemisia Bellante might be the most alluring young woman he'd met in a long time but a deal was a deal and his word was his word. Their paper marriage would last six months and no longer. Nonno's doctors had given him no more than a year to live if he didn't start treatment soon. The clock was ticking on the old man's life and Luca was determined to present him with the perfect choice of bride.

The housekeeper led him to the same salon as yesterday, where Artemisia was waiting for him standing by the windows. Her hands were clasped behind her back, her posture guarded. She looked regal and elegant even though she was wearing casual clothes—blue jeans and a white shirt with a patterned scarf draped artfully around her neck. The jeans highlighted the shapely curves of her hips and the white shirt brought out the creamy tone of her skin. Her chin was at a proud height, her deep brown eyes shining with unmistakable dislike.

Hot and heavy desire tingled in his groin. Her dislike of him was a bigger turn-on than he'd expected. Dating had become a little too easy for him lately—a little too boring and predictable. But nothing about Artemisia Bellante was boring or predictable.

Rein it in, buddy. You're not going there, remember?

Luca gave a sweeping bow. '*Buongiorno*, Artemisia. Have you made your decision?'

Her indrawn breath was like the hiss of a cornered cat. 'I have.'

'And?' Luca was only conscious of holding his breath when his lungs began to tighten. He wanted her as his bride. No one else was going to do. He *had* to have *her*. He couldn't explain his intractable stance other than that something about her ticked all the boxes.

She held his gaze with her icy one, her jaw set, her colour high. 'I will marry you.'

The relief that swept through him momentarily caught him off guard. It wasn't that he'd expected her to say no but somehow he hadn't realised until now how *much* he'd wanted her to say yes. 'Good. I'm glad you see the sense in doing so.'

Her eyebrows rose ever so slightly above her glittering eyes. 'However, I have some conditions on my acceptance of your offer.'

Luca was not one to allow people to push him around but something about her expression made him make an exception. She stirred him in a way he had never been stirred before. His blood heated with a backbeat of desire, his nostrils flaring to take in the flowery scent of her perfume. 'Go on.'

She unfolded her arms and smoothed her hands down the front of her thighs. He ran his gaze down the slim length of her legs and her neat calves. She was wearing light brown suede ankle boots that gave her an inch or two more height. But even with the benefit of heels, she still wouldn't make it to the top of his shoulder. But that wasn't the only thing she was wearing—his grandmother's engagement ring winked proudly, almost defiantly, on her left hand. The arabesque design chosen so lovingly by his *nonno* to give to the love of his life—Luca's grandmother—suited Artemisia's hand as if designed especially for her. A faint alarm bell sounded at the back of his mind. He would have to be extra careful to keep his emotions out of this arrangement. Their relationship was a business deal and nothing more. There was no point feeling a little sentimental about seeing his grandmother's ring on Artie's hand. There was nothing sentimental about his choice of engagement ring. Sure, he could have bought any other ring but he had deliberately used his *nonna*'s ring knowing it would add authenticity to his committed relationship status in the eyes of his grandfather.

It was his grandfather who was sentimental.

Not him.

'Won't you sit down?' Artie's tone was all cool politeness but her eyes were hard with bitterness.

Luca gestured to the sofa nearest her. 'Ladies first.'

Artie drew in another sharp breath and sat on the sofa, her hands clasped around her crossed knee, her plump mouth tightly set. 'So, I've decided to accept your offer on the proviso we're married here at the *castello*. A quiet wedding, minimal guests.'

It intrigued him why she wanted a low-key wedding. Didn't most young women want to be a princess for the day? He could think of at least half a dozen of his ex-lovers who had dropped enormous hints about their dream wedding. It had killed his interest in them stone-dead. 'Is there any particular reason why you want to be married here and not at one of the local churches?'

Her gaze didn't quite meet his but aimed for the top of his left shoulder. 'My father's funeral was held here, so too was my mother's. It's where many of my ancestors are buried.'

'*Sì*, but a funeral is a little different from a wedding, is it not?'

Her clear brown gaze collided with his. 'Not from my perspective. This isn't a real marriage. I would be uncomfortable desecrating a church by saying vows neither of us intends to keep. It would be disrespectful. Nor do I want a big, flashy wedding with people I don't know and have nothing in common with attending. It would be a waste of money and effort.'

Luca didn't care where they were married as long as they were married. He only hoped Nonno would be well enough to be able to travel from his home in Tuscany, but, since Umbria was a neighbouring region, it wasn't a long journey—just over two hours' drive.

'Fine. We'll marry here. Leave the arrangements to me. I've already applied for a licence so we don't have to wait the six weeks normally required. Your father sent me a copy of your birth certificate and passport before he died. I took the liberty of getting things on the move.'

Her eyes widened and her mouth fell open.

'You were so sure I would accept? But you hadn't even met me in person until yesterday.'

He shrugged one shoulder. 'Your father showed me a photo and he talked about you a lot. I was satisfied you would be suitable.'

She uncrossed her legs and sprang off the sofa, moving some distance away. 'I would have thought a man in your position wouldn't have to resort to finding a mail-order bride.' Scorn underlined every word she spoke. 'What if I'd said no?'

Luca gave a slow smile. 'I would have found some way to change your mind.'

Her chin came up and her eyes flashed. 'I can't believe my father encouraged you in this ridiculous mission to acquire a wife. When did you meet with him? I've never seen you come here before yesterday and I barely left my father's side.'

'I visited your father when he was in hospital with pneumonia late last year. He talked you up so much it intrigued me. I was disappointed not to see you on one of my visits but he said you weren't keen on hospitals since the accident. We emailed or phoned after that.'

She bit her lip and looked away. 'Did he say anything else about me?'

'Just that you were shy and not much of a party girl.'

She gave a snort of humourless laughter. 'Yes, well, that's certainly true.'

Luca rose from the sofa and walked over to a row of picture frames on a sideboard. He picked up a photo taken when Artie was a child, sitting on her mother's knee. 'Your mother was very beautiful. She was English, *si*?'

'Y-yes…' There was a slight catch in her voice.

Luca put the photo back on the sideboard and turned to face her. 'It's hard to lose a parent in your teens, especially the same sex parent.' Harder still when you were the cause of their death. And the death of your only brother. The guilt never left him. It sat on his shoulder. It followed him. It prodded him. It never let him forget. It kept him awake at night. His own personal stalker, torturing him with the what-ifs and the if-onlys.

Her brown eyes met his. 'You lost your father and older brother when you were a teenager, didn't you?'

Luca knew there was still stuff about his father and brother's death online. Not so easy to come across these days but it was still there if you did a thorough enough search. It had been a big news story at the time due to his father's high profile in business circles.

He could still see the headlines now— *Property developer CEO and son and heir lost in heavy surf in Argentina.*

There had been nothing about Luca's role in their drowning and he only found out years later it was because his *nonno* had pulled some strings in order to protect him.

Another reason his marriage to Artie had to go ahead and soon. He owed his *nonno* peace in this last stage of his life.

'Yes. When I was thirteen.' He stripped his voice of all emotion—he could have been discussing the stock exchange instead of the worst day of his life.

'I'm sorry.' Artie waited a beat and added, 'Is your mother still alive?'

'Yes. She lives in New York now.'

'Has she remarried?'

'No.'

There was a silence.

Luca could have filled it with all the reasons why his mother no longer lived in Italy. Her unrelenting grief. His strained relationship with her that nothing he said or did could fix. The constant triggers being around him caused her. The empty hole in her life that nothing could fill. The hole he had created by his actions on that fateful day. He hadn't just lost his father and brother on that day—he'd lost his entire family as he'd known it. Even his grandparents—as caring and supportive as they tried to be—had been sideswiped by grief and became shadows of their former selves. His extended family—aunts, uncles, cousins—all of them had been affected by his actions that day.

'So, what changed your mind about marrying me?' Luca decided it was safer to stay on the topic of their upcoming marriage rather than drift into territory he wanted left well alone. 'Let me guess. Was it the engagement ring?'

She swallowed, her cheeks blooming with colour. 'In a way, yes.'

Luca hadn't taken her for a gold-digger but it was a damn fine ring. His eyes flicked to her left hand. 'It looks good on you. But I hope you don't mind it being second hand. It belonged to my grandmother. She left it to me in her will.'

Her eyes widened to the size of dinner plates. 'Your grandmother's? Oh, my goodness. Just as well I—' She bit her lip and shifted her gaze a fraction, the colour in her cheeks deepening.

'Just as well you…?' Luca prompted, intrigued by her cagey expression.

Her slim throat rose and fell over a swallow and her gaze slipped out of reach of his. 'I—I misplaced it for a couple of hours. But it's your fault for giving me such a ridiculously valuable ring. A priceless heirloom, for pity's sake. What on earth were you thinking? Of course, I'll give it back to you once the six months is up.'

'I don't want it back. It's a gift.'

Her gaze flicked back to his, shock written all over her features. 'I couldn't possibly keep it. It's worth a small fortune, not to mention the sentimental value.'

Luca shrugged. 'It's no skin off my nose what you do with it once our marriage is over. It's just a ring. I will have no further use for it after this. It means nothing to me.'

Her mouth tightened. 'Is there anything that means something to you other than making disgusting amounts of money?'

Luca slanted his mouth into a cynical smile. 'There isn't a law against being successful in business. Money opens a lot of doors.'

'I would imagine it closes others. How

would you know if people liked you for you or for your wealth?'

'I'm a good judge of character. I soon weed out the timewasters and hangers-on.'

Her top lip curled and her eyes shone with loathing. 'Well, bully for you.'

CHAPTER THREE

ARTIE WOULDN'T HAVE admitted it even under torture, but she was getting off on sparring with Luca Ferrantelli. Every time they exchanged words, little bubbles of excitement trickled into her bloodstream. He was intelligent and quick-witted and charming and she had to keep on her toes to keep up with him.

She couldn't understand why he had given her his grandmother's engagement ring. *Eek!* Just as well she hadn't lost it. But he didn't seem all that attached to the stunning piece of jewellery, and yet she had fallen in love with it at first sight. Surely he had at least one sentimental bone in his body, or was everything just another business deal?

Luca's brief mention of his father and brother intrigued her. Mostly because he seemed reluctant to dwell on the subject. His expression had given little away, his flat, emotionless tone even less. But still, she sensed there was pain beneath the surface—deep pain that made him distance himself from it whenever he could.

Maybe Rosa was right—Luca Ferrantelli had more than a few layers to his personality that begged to be explored.

But Artie knew all too well about deep emotional pain. Talking about her mother, thinking about the accident and its aftermath sent her into a spiral of despair. Guilt was her constant companion. Wasn't it her fault her father had lost control of his finances? He hadn't been the same after the accident. Losing Artie's mother, and losing the use of his legs as well as an acquired brain injury, had meant he was not the same man—nor ever could be—and she was entirely to blame. Nothing Artie could do would ever change that. It was only fitting that she wed Luca Ferrantelli and reclaim her family's heritage.

It was her penance. The price she must pay. But she would make the best out of the situation by owning her choice to marry Luca rather than feel he had forced her hand.

'We need to discuss the honeymoon.' Luca's expression was inscrutable. 'Do you have somewhere you'd like to go?'

Honeymoon?

Artie widened her eyes so far she thought they might pop right out of her head. She clasped her hand to her throat where her heart now seemed to be lodged. 'A…a honeymoon? Whatever for? You said it's going to be a marriage in name only. Why would we need to go on a honeymoon?' Even saying the word 'honeymoon' made her body go all tingly and her heart race and her blood heat. Heat that stormed into her cheeks and simmered in other more secret places.

One of his dark eyebrows lifted at her stuttering protest, a satirical glint shining in his gaze. 'I'm fine with a quiet wedding here at the *castello* but I insist on a honeymoon. It will give our marriage more credibility if we are seen to go away together for a short break.'

Seen? In public? Be in wide open spaces? Rushing crowds. Traffic. Noise. Busyness. Artie stumbled backwards, her arms wrapping around her body, her breathing tight and laboured. 'No. I can't do that. I don't want to go. There's no need. It's not a proper marriage and it's wrong of you to insist on it.'

Breathe. Breathe. Breathe.

Luca frowned. 'Are you worried I'll take

advantage of you? Please be assured that is not going to happen. I gave you my word.'

'I don't want to go anywhere with you,' Artie said. 'How could you think I would? I don't even like you.'

His eyes dipped to her mouth then back to her gaze. 'Artemisia, we need to be seen together in public. It's not going to work unless we present as a normal couple. We'll have to live together most, if not all, of the time.'

Her stomach turned over. 'L-live together?'

'But of course. Isn't that what husbands and wives do?'

Artie gulped. Her skin prickled, her legs trembled, her mind raced. Live with Luca Ferrantelli? What would that entail? She couldn't even leave her own home. How on earth would she move into his? Should she tell him about her social phobia? Would he understand? No. Not likely. Few people did. Even the professionals who had visited her at the *castello* had more or less given up on her.

Her gaze moved out of reach of his and she fiddled with the sleeve of her shirt for something to do with her hands. 'I'm sorry, but couldn't you move in here? I mean, this place is huge and you can have your own suite of rooms and we'd hardly have to see each other and no one would ever know we're not—'

'No.' His tone was so adamant the word could have been underlined in thick black ink.

Artie swung away from him, trying to get her breathing back under control. She was light-headed and nauseous, her stomach churning fast enough to make butter. She was going to faint… No, she wasn't. She was going to fight it. Fight *him*. She took a deep breath and turned around to face him. 'I will *not* leave my home. Not for you. A marriage of convenience is supposed to be convenient for both parties. It's not convenient for me to move right now. I've only just buried my father. I'd like more time to…to spend grieving out of the view of the public.' It wasn't completely a lie. She missed her father, not because they were particularly close but because looking after him had given structure and purpose to her life.

Luca studied her for a long moment, his expression giving nothing away. She tried not to squirm under his unnerving scrutiny but it was a mammoth effort and only added to her light-headedness. 'All right. We'll delay the honeymoon.'

Relief swept through her and she brushed back her hair from her face, her hand not quite as steady as she would have liked. 'Thank you.'

She hadn't been in a car since coming home from hospital after the accident. She hadn't been in a plane or train or bus since she was fifteen. She hadn't been around more than two or three people in a decade. Her life was contained within these four ancient stone walls and she couldn't see it changing any time soon.

Luca closed the distance between them and held her gaze for another beat or two. 'I realise your father's financial situation has come as a shock to you. And I understand how resistant you are to my plan to turn things to your advantage. But I want my grandfather to see us married and living as a couple.'

'Why is that so important to you?'

'He's got cancer but he won't agree to treatment.'

'Oh… I'm sorry.'

Luca ran a hand down his face, the sound of his palm scraping over his regrowth loud in the silence. 'Unless he has treatment soon, he will die within a year. His dream has always been to see me settled down with a nice young woman. He disapproves of my casual approach to relationships and has been at pains to let me know at every opportunity. I want him to find a reason to live, knowing I've found a suitable bride.'

A suitable bride.

If only Luca knew how unsuitable she really was. Would he still want to marry her if he knew the truth about her? 'Will your grandfather be well enough to come here for the wedding?'

'I hope so.'

Artie bit her lip. She was conflicted about keeping her social anxiety from Luca but neither could she risk losing her home if he decided to withdraw his offer of marriage. She didn't know him well enough to trust he would make allowances for her. He'd already told her he was a ruthless businessman who didn't allow emotion to cloud his judgement. How could she hope he might be understanding and compassionate about her mental health issues? 'But you only know me as my father presented me. I might be the worst person in the world.'

A lazy smile tilted his mouth and his eyes darkened. 'I like what I've seen so far.'

Artie could feel colour pouring into her

cheeks. Could feel a faint hollow ache building, beating between her thighs. Could feel a light tingling in her breasts. His gaze went to her mouth and she couldn't stop herself from sweeping them with the tip of her tongue. His eyes followed the movement of her tongue and liquid warmth spread through her core like warmed treacle. What invisible chemistry was doing this to her? What potent force did Luca Ferrantelli have over her? She had never been so aware of another person. Never so aware of her own body. Her senses were on high alert, her pulse racing.

Suddenly he wasn't standing a metre away but was close enough for her to smell the sharp, clean citrus notes of his aftershave. Had he moved or had she?

She looked into the depths of his gaze and her heart skipped a beat. And another. And another, until it felt like tiny racing footsteps were pounding against the membrane surrounding her heart.

He lifted his hand to her face, trailing his index finger down the slope of her cheek from just above her ear down to the base of her chin. Every nerve in her skin exploded with sensation. Every pore acutely sensitive to his faintest touch.

'You are much more beautiful in person than in the photo your father showed me.' Luca's tone was a bone-melting blend of rough and smooth. Honey and gravel. Temptation and danger.

Artie couldn't take her eyes off his mouth, drawn by a force as old as time. Male and female desire meeting. Wanting. Needing. Tempting. 'I don't get called Artemisia... most people call me Artie.'

Oh, for pity's sake. Couldn't you think of something a little more sophisticated to say?

Luca gave a crooked smile and something warm spread through her chest. 'Artie. It's cute. I like it. Artemisia, Queen of Halicarnassus. She was an ally of the Persian King Xerces in 430 BCE and reputedly brave in battle.'

That's me—brave. Not.

'My mother chose it. She loved Greek history.'

His gaze became hooded and he glanced at her mouth again. 'There will be times when we'll be expected to show affection towards one another. Are you going to be okay with that?'

'W-what sort of affection?'

'Kissing. Holding hands. Touching.'

Her lower body began to throb with a strange kind of ache. She couldn't stop herself thinking about places he might touch her—places that were already tingling in anticipation. How would she cope with a casual brush of his hand? His strong arm around her waist? His mouth pressed to hers? No one had ever touched her with a lover's touch. No one had ever kissed her. The desire to be touched by him was overwhelming. Her body craved it like a drug.

'Okay.'

Okay? Are you out of your mind?

Artie *was* out of her mind—with lust. She had never felt so out of control of her body. It was acting of its own volition, responding to him in ways she had never expected. She didn't even like him. He was arrogant and confident in a way she found irritating. It was as if he expected her to throw herself at him just like any other woman he had encountered. How was she going to resist him if he kissed her? How would it feel to have that firm mouth moving against hers?

Luca continued to look at her with a heart-stopping intensity. 'If you don't want me to kiss you then you need to tell me, because right now I can think of nothing I want to do more.' His voice lowered to a deep bass that sent another wave of heat coursing through her body.

'What makes you think I want you to kiss me now? What would be the point? There's no one here but us.' Artie was proud of her calm and collected tone when inside her body was steaming, simmering, smouldering.

His thumb pressed lightly on the middle of her bottom lip, sending tingles down the length of her spine. 'The way you're looking at me.'

'How am I looking at you?'

Eek. Was that her voice? She had to do something about her voice. None of that whispery, husky rubbish. She had to be brusque and matter-of-fact.

'You must be imagining it.'

He cupped one side of her face with his hand, the slight roughness of his palm making her insides coil and tighten with lust. 'Maybe.' He gave a quick on-off smile and dropped his hand from her face. 'So, the wedding. How does this weekend sound?'

Artie only just managed to suppress a gasp. '*This* weekend? What's the rush?'

'I'm not a fan of long engagements.'

'Funny. But how am I going to find a dress

in time? Or are you expecting me to turn up naked?'

Argh. Why did you say that?

A dark glint came into his eyes. 'Now, there's an idea.'

Artie pursed her lips, hoping her cheeks were not glowing as hot as they felt. 'I can safely say I will never, ever be naked in front of you.'

He glided a lazy finger down her burning cheek, a smile in his eyes. 'Have you been naked in front of anyone?'

Artie stepped back, annoyed with herself for not doing so earlier. She *had* to keep her distance. It was dangerous to stand so close to him. She had so little immunity to his sensual power. She had to remember he was a powerful magnet and she was a tiny iron filing.

'I'm not going to discuss my private life with you. It's none of your damn business.'

'We have to know a few things about each other otherwise no one will accept our marriage as the real thing.'

Artie frowned. 'What? Are you going to pretend you're in love with me or something? Who's going to believe it? We're total opposites.'

'Ah, but don't they say opposites attract?' His smile melted her bones—she could feel her legs trembling to keep her upright.

Artie compressed her lips and iced her gaze. 'This may come as a surprise to a man with an ego the size of yours but I'm not attracted to you.'

He gave a deep chuckle. 'Then you're going to have to call on every bit of acting power you possess to convince my grandfather otherwise. Think you can do that, *cara mia*?'

The Italian endearment almost made her swoon. She hoisted her chin. 'Do you, Mr Hardened Cynical Playboy, think *you* can act like a man passionately in love with his bride?'

His gaze held hers in a smouldering lock that made the backs of her knees tingle. 'That will be the easy part.'

CHAPTER FOUR

ARTIE STOOD IN FRONT of the cheval mirror in her bedroom and checked her appearance. She had decided against wearing her mother's wedding dress and chosen a cream satin ball-gown of her mother's instead. It was a classic design with a tulle underskirt that emphasised her neat waist, and a close-fitting bodice that hinted at the shape of her breasts without revealing too much cleavage. She hadn't wanted to taint her mother's beautiful wedding gown with her charade of a marriage. Her parents had married for love and lived happily together until Artie insisted on going to a birthday party against their wishes when she was fifteen.

She bit down on her lip until it hurt. Why had she been so adamant about going to that stupid party? Where were those supposed friends of hers now? Only a handful came to visit her in hospital. None had come to the *castello* once she had been released. None had come to her mother's funeral. She had stood beside her father's wheelchair as her mother was lowered into the family plot at the *castello* with her heart in pieces, guilt raining down on her heavier than what was coming from the dismal sky above. How could one teenage decision have so many unforeseen consequences?

Artie plucked at the skirt of her dress, her stomach an ants' nest of nerves. Today was her wedding day. The day she married Luca Ferrantelli in a paper marriage to save her family home. Would this be another decision she would later regret? Or would the consolation of getting the *castello* back into her possession wipe out any misgivings? She glanced at the engagement ring on her hand. The longer she wore it, the more she loved it. She felt strangely connected to Luca's grandmother by wearing her ring. But would the old lady spin in her grave to know Artie was entering into a loveless union with her grandson?

Rosa came in carrying a bouquet of flowers she had picked from the garden. 'You look beautiful, Artie.' She handed her the simple but fragrant bouquet. 'You're not wearing a veil?'

Artie brought the flowers up to her nose and breathed in the heady scent of roses and orange blossom. 'This isn't a proper wedding.'

Rosa frowned. 'But it's still a legal one. You might as well look like a proper bride. And make that handsome groom of yours sit up and take notice.' She went to the large wardrobe and pulled out the long cardboard box where Artie's mother's wedding dress and veil were stored on the top shelf. She placed the box on the bed and lifted the lid and removed the tissue-wrapped heirloom hand-embroidered veil that had been worn by both Artie's mother and grandmother. Rosa shook out the veil and then brought it over to Artie. 'Come on. Indulge me.'

Artie rolled her eyes but gave in, allowing Rosa to fasten the veil on her head, securing it with hair pins. Rosa draped the veil over Artie's face and then stepped back to inspect her handiwork. 'You will knock Luca Ferrantelli's socks off, *si*?'

Artie turned back to look at her reflection. She did indeed look like a proper bride. She glanced at Rosa. 'Tell me I'm not making the biggest mistake of my life. My second biggest, I mean.'

Rosa grasped one of Artie's hands, her eyes shimmering with tears. 'You have already lost so much. You can't lose the *castello* as well. Sometimes we have to do whatever it takes to make the best of things.' She released Artie's hand and brushed at her eyes and gave a rueful smile. 'Weddings always make me emotional. Just as well I didn't get married myself.'

'Would you have liked to?' Artie was surprised she hadn't thought to ask before now. Rosa was in her sixties and had been a part of the *castello* household for as long as Artie could remember. They had talked about many things over the years but not about the housekeeper's love life or lack thereof.

Rosa made a business of fussing over the arrangement of the skirt of Artie's gown. 'I fell in love once a long time ago. It didn't work out.'

'What happened?'

Rosa bent down lower to pick a fallen rose petal off the floor. She scrunched it in her hand and gave a thin-lipped smile. 'He married someone else. I never found anyone else who measured up.'

'Oh, that's so sad.'

Rosa laughed but it sounded tinny. 'I saved myself a lot of heartache. Apparently, he's been divorced three times since then.' Her expression suddenly sobered. 'Your parents were lucky to have found each other. I know they didn't have as long together as they would have liked but it's better to have five years with the right one than fifty with the wrong one.'

But what about six months with a man who had only met her a matter of days ago? A man who was so dangerously attractive, her blood raced every time he looked at her?

Luca stood in the *castello*'s chapel, waiting for Artie to appear. His grandfather had been too unwell to travel, but Luca planned to take his new bride to meet him as soon as their marriage was official. Luca had organised for a priest to officiate rather than a celebrant, because he knew it would please his grandfather, who was a deeply religious man—hence his disapproval of Luca's life in the fast lane.

As much as he wanted his grandfather to meet Artie as soon as possible, he was quite glad he would have her to himself for a day or two. They would hardly be convincing as a newly married couple if they didn't look comfortable and at ease with each other.

She was a challenge he was tempted to take on. Her resistance to his charm was potently attractive. Not because he didn't respect and honour the word no when a woman said it. He could take rejection and take it well. He was never so emotionally invested in a relationship that he was particularly cut up when it ended.

But he sensed Artie's interest in him. Sensed the chemistry that swirled in the atmosphere when they were together. Would it be risky to explore that chemistry? She was young and unworldly. What if she didn't accept the terms of the deal and wanted more than he was prepared to give? He couldn't allow that to happen. If she fell in love with him it would change everything.

And if he fell in love with her...

He sidestepped the thought like someone avoiding a sinkhole. Loving her would indeed be a pitfall. For her and for him. Love was a dangerous emotion. Whenever he thought of the possibility of loving someone, his heart would shy away like a horse refusing a jump. Too dangerous. Too risky. Too painful.

The back of Luca's neck started to tingle

and he turned to see Artie standing in the portal. He suppressed a gasp, his eyes drinking in the vision of her dressed in a stunning cream ballgown and off-white heirloom veil. The bright golden sunlight backlit her slim frame, making her look like an angel. As she walked towards him carrying a small bouquet of flowers he had to remind himself to breathe. The closer she got, the more his heart pounded, the more his blood thundered. And a strange sensation flowed into his chest. Warmth spreading over something hard and frozen, melting, reshaping, softening.

He gave himself a mental slap. No emotions allowed. This was a business deal. Nothing else. So what if she looked as beautiful as an angel? So what if his body roared with lust at the thought of touching her? This wasn't about him—it was about his grandfather. Giving him the will to live long enough to have treatment that could cure him or at least give him a few more precious years of life.

Artie came to stand beside him, her face behind the veil composed, and yet twin circles of pink glowed in her cheeks. Her makeup highlighted the flawless, creamy texture of her skin, the deep brown of her eyes and the thick ink-black lashes that surrounded them.

Her lips shone with a hint of lip gloss, making him ache to press his mouth to hers to see if it tasted as sweet and luscious as it looked. He could smell her perfume, an intoxicating blend of fresh flowers that reminded him of the sweet hope of spring after a long, bleak winter.

'You look breathtaking,' Luca said, taking her hands in his. Her small fingers moved within the embrace of his and a lightning rod of lust almost knocked him off his feet. Maybe he shouldn't have suggested a paper marriage. Maybe he should have insisted on the real deal. The thought of consummating their marriage sent a wave of heat through his body. But his conscience slammed on the brakes. No. No. No. It wouldn't be fair. He wasn't the settling-down type and she had fairy-tale romance written all over her. Which, ironically, was why she was perfect for the role of his temporary bride. No one else would satisfy his grandfather. It *had* to be her.

'I—I'm nervous…' Her voice trembled and her teeth sank into the plush softness of her bottom lip.

Luca gently squeezed her fingers. 'Don't be.' His voice was so deep and rough it sounded like it had come from the centre of the earth. He didn't like admitting it, but he was nervous too. Not about repeating the vows and signing the register—those were formalities he could easily compartmentalise in his brain. He was worried his promise to keep their relationship on paper was going to be the real kicker. He gave her hand another light squeeze and smiled. 'Let's do this.'

And they turned to face the priest and the service began…

'I, Artemisia Elisabetta, take you, Luca Benedetto, to be my husband…' Artie repeated her vows with a slight quaver in her voice. 'I promise to be true to you in good times and bad, in sickness and in health.' She swallowed and continued, conscious of Luca's dark gaze holding hers, 'I will love and honour you all the days of my life.'

She wasn't a particularly religious person but saying words she didn't mean made her wonder if she was in danger of a lightning strike. The only lightning strike she had suffered so far had been the tingling zap coursing through her body when Luca first took her hand. Every cell of her body was aware of him. Dressed in a mid-blue morning suit, he looked like he had just stepped off a billboard advertisement for designer menswear. She could smell the lemon and lime of his aftershave—it teased her nostrils, sending her senses into a tailspin. How could a man smell so damn delicious?

Eek! How could a man look so damn attractive?

Double eek! How could she be marrying him?

Luca's hand took her left one and slipped on the wedding ring as he repeated his vows. 'I, Luca Benedetto, take you, Artemisia Elisabetta, to be my wife. I promise to be true to you in good times and bad, in sickness and in health.' He paused for a beat and continued with a rough edge to his voice, 'I will love and honour you all the days of my life.'

Artie blinked back moisture gathering in her eyes. He sounded so convincing. He even looked convincing with his gaze so focused on her, his mouth smiling at her as if she was the most amazing woman who had ever walked upon the face of the earth.

It's an act. Don't be fooled by it. None of this means anything to him and neither should it mean anything to you.

'You may kiss the bride.'

The priest's words startled Artie out of her reverie and she only had time to snatch in a breath before Luca's hands settled on her hips and drew her closer, his mouth descending inexorably towards hers. The first warm, firm press of his lips sent a jolt of electricity through her body. A jolt that travelled all the way down her spine and fizzed like a sparkler deep in her core. He lifted his lips off hers for an infinitesimal moment as if time had suddenly paused. Then he brought his mouth back to hers and sensations rippled through her as his lips moved against hers with increasing pressure, his hands on her hips bringing her even closer to the hard heat of his stirring body.

One of his hands left her hip to cradle one side of her face, his touch gentle, almost reverent, and yet his mouth was pure sin. Tempting, teasing, tantalising. She opened to him and his tongue touched hers and her insides quaked and throbbed with longing. She pressed closer, her arms going around his neck, her senses reeling as his tongue invited hers in an erotic dance. Every nerve in her lips and mouth awakened to his kiss, flowering open like soft petals to strong sunshine. She became aware of her body in a way she never had before—its needs, urges, flagrantly responding to the dark primal call of his.

Luca angled his head to change position, his tongue stroking against hers, a low, deep groan sounding in his throat. It thrilled her to know he was as undone by their kiss as she was. Thrilled and excited her to realise her own sensual power. Power she hadn't known she possessed until now.

The priest cleared his throat and Luca pulled back from her with a dazed look on his face. Artie suspected she was looking just as shell-shocked as him. Her mouth felt swollen, her feminine core agitated with a roaring hunger he alone had awakened.

Luca blinked a couple of times as if to reset his equilibrium. 'Well, hello there, Signora Ferrantelli.' His voice was rusty, his gaze drifting to her mouth as if he couldn't quite believe what had happened between them moments before.

Artie licked her lips and tasted the salty sexiness of his. 'Hello…'

Luca spoke briefly to the priest, thanking him for his services, and then led Artie to where Rosa had set up refreshments in the garden. She sensed him pulling up a drawbridge, a pulling back into himself. He stood without touching her, his expression inscrutable.

'Right. Time to celebrate. And then tomorrow we'll go and visit my grandfather.'

A wave of ice-cold dread washed over her. 'But can't we leave it a while? I mean, wouldn't he expect us to be on our honeymoon and—?'

'I can't afford to leave it too long before I introduce you to him,' Luca said, frowning. 'He's in a vulnerable state of health.'

Artie chewed at her lip and lowered her gaze. 'I understand all that but I need more time to get used to being your…wife. I'm worried I'll do or say something that will make your grandfather suspicious.'

Luca gave her a smouldering look. 'If you kiss me like you did just then, any doubts he has will disappear.'

Artie could feel her cheeks firing up. 'I was only following your lead. I haven't been kissed before, so—'

'Really?' His eyebrows shot up in surprise.

She pulled away from him and hugged her arms around her body. 'Go on, mock me for being a twenty-five-year-old virgin. I must seem like a pariah to someone like you who changes lovers daily.'

Her conscience rolled its eyes. *I can't believe you just told him you're a virgin.*

He scraped a hand through his hair, making it tousled. 'Look, I kind of figured from your father that you were lacking in experience but I didn't realise you've never had a boyfriend, even as a teenager. Did your father forbid you from going out or something?'

Artie averted her gaze. 'No. I was busy looking after him after the accident that killed my mother and seriously injured him. There wasn't time for dating.'

His deep frown brought his dark eyebrows together. 'Why were you the one looking after him? Why didn't he employ a nurse or carer?'

Artie turned slightly so she was facing the view over the estate. Luca's penetrating gaze was too unsettling, too unnerving. How could she explain her reasons for taking care of her father? How could she explain the guilt that had chained her to his side? The guilt that still plagued her and had led her to marry Luca in order to save her family's home? The home that was the only thing she had left of her family. 'It was my choice to look after him. I was happy to do it.'

Luca came up behind her and placed his hands on the tops of her shoulders and turned her to face him. He expression was still etched in a frown, his hazel eyes gentle with concern. 'You were just a child when the accident occurred. It was unfair of your father to allow you to sacrifice yourself in such a way. But what about school? Surely you would have had plenty of opportunity to mix with people your own age?'

Artie pressed her lips together for a moment. 'I finished my education online. I was given special permission. I didn't want to leave my father to the care of strangers. He was stricken with grief after losing my mother. We both were. It was my choice to take care of him—no one forced me to do it.'

His hands began a gentle massaging movement that made the tense muscles in her neck and shoulders melt like snow under warm sunshine. 'I think what you did for your father was admirable and yet I can't help feeling he exploited you. You should've had more time to yourself doing all the things teenagers and young adults do.'

Artie stepped out of his hold and interlaced her fingers in front of her body. She glanced to where Rosa was hovering with a bottle of champagne. 'Shouldn't we be mingling with Father Pasquale and our two other guests?' She didn't wait for him to answer and turned and walked towards the housekeeper standing with the priest and the other witness, who worked part-time on the Castello Mireille estate.

Luca watched Artie pick up a glass of champagne from the silver tray the housekeeper was holding. Her expression was now coolly composed but he sensed he had pressed on a nerve when discussing her role of caring for her father. He'd already suspected she was a virgin—her father had intimated as such—but no way had he suspected she had zero experience when it came to dating.

No one had kissed her before him.

She had never had a boyfriend, not even during her teens. How had her father allowed that to happen? Surely he must have realised his daughter was missing out on socialising with people her age?

Luca ran his tongue over his lips and tasted the sweet, fruity residue of her lip gloss. He could still feel the soft imprint of her lips on his, could still feel the throb of desire kissing her had evoked in his body, the deep pulses in his groin, the tingles in his thighs and lower spine.

He had kissed many women, too many to recall in any detail, but he knew he would never forget his first kiss with Artie. It was embedded in his memory. He could recall every contour of her soft mouth, every brush and glide of her tongue, her sweet vanilla and wild-strawberry taste.

But he would have to find some way to forget, for theirs was to be a paper marriage. A six-month time frame to achieve his goal of setting his grandfather's mind at peace. Knowing Artie had so little experience was an even bigger reason to stick to his plan of a hands-off arrangement. It wouldn't be fair to explore the physical chemistry between them, because it might raise her expectations on their relationship.

He didn't *do* relationships. And certainly not *that* type of relationship.

Long-term relationships required commitment and responsibility for the health and safety of your partner. His track record on keeping those he loved safe was appalling. It was easier not to love. Easier to keep his emotions in check, to freeze them so deep inside himself they could never be thawed. To imagine oneself falling in love just because of a bit of scorching hot chemistry was a foolish and reckless thing to do. He no longer did anything reckless and foolish.

Luca glanced at Artie and something pinched in his chest. She was standing next to the ancient stone fountain, the tinkling of water and the sound of birds chirping in the shrubbery a perfect backdrop for her old-world beauty. The sunlight brought out the glossy sheen of her dark brown hair, the light breeze playing with a curl that had worked its way loose from her elegant up-do. She was looking into the distance, a small frown on her forehead, and every now and again the tip of her tongue came out and swept across her lips where his had recently pressed. She turned her head and caught him staring at her, and her cheeks pooled with a delicate shade of pink.

Had he made a mistake in choosing her to be his temporary bride? She was so innocent, so untouched and other-worldly, like she had been transported from another time in history or straight out of a classic fairy tale. And yet he'd felt a connection with her from the moment he met her. A powerful connection that no amount of logic and rationality could dismiss. His brain said *Don't go there* and yet his body roared with primal hunger.

But he would have to get his self-control back in shape, and fast, because falling for his sweet and innocent bride would be the most reckless and foolish thing of all.

CHAPTER FIVE

Artie was aware of Luca's gaze resting on her every time she glanced his way. Aware of the way her body responded to his lightest touch. The merest brush of his fingers set off spot fires in her flesh, sending heat travelling to every secret place in her body. Smouldering there like hot coals just waiting for a breath of oxygen to fan them into vibrant life.

His kiss...

Best not to think too much about his kiss. They were supposed to be keeping their relationship platonic, but nothing about Luca's kiss was platonic. It was sensory overload and she wondered if she would ever recover. Or stop wanting him to kiss her again. And why stop at kisses? He had woken something in her, something hungry and needy that begged to be assuaged. The idea of asking Luca to tweak the rules of their marriage slipped into her mind like an uninvited guest. It would be an ideal opportunity for her to get some experience on board. A six-month marriage where she could indulge in the delights of the flesh. What was there to lose other than her virginity?

Your pride? her conscience piped up. *He can have anyone. You're not even his type. How do you think you could ever satisfy him for six minutes, let alone six months?*

Luca took a glass of champagne off Rosa and came over to where Artie was standing near the fountain. He glanced towards the priest and then back to her. 'Father Pasquale is having a good time indulging in Rosa's food. How long has she been working here?'

'Since I was a baby,' Artie said. 'This is her home as much as it is mine.'

'So, what would she do if you were to sell up and move away?'

Artie raised her chin. 'I would never sell the *castello*. And I don't want to live anywhere but here.'

I can't live anywhere but here.

Luca held her gaze for a long moment. 'How will you maintain the estate? It needs a lot of work, and sooner rather than later.'

She drained her champagne glass and sent

him a narrowed glance. 'Is this the right time to discuss this? It's our wedding day.'

His brows drew together in a frown. 'Do I have to remind you of the terms of our marriage?'

'No.' She flashed him a pointed look. 'Do *you* need reminding? That kiss was a little enthusiastic for someone who insisted on keeping things on paper.'

His gaze went to her mouth, and the atmosphere throbbed with heightened intensity. 'Maybe, but it wasn't a one-way kiss, was it, *cara*? You were with me all the way.' His tone was so deep and rough it sent a tingle down her spine. And his eyes contained a glint that made something warm and liquid spill between her thighs.

Artie went to swing away from him but his hand came down on her arm. A shiver coursed through her body at the feel of his long, strong, tanned fingers encircling her wrist. She looked down at his hand on her flesh and the warm, liquid sensation in her lower body spread like fire throughout her pelvis. She lifted her gaze to his and raised her eyebrows in a haughty manner. 'W-what are you doing?' Her tone was breathless rather than offended.

His broad thumb began a slow caress over the pulse point on her wrist, the fast-paced throb of her blood betraying her even further. She breathed in the scent of him—the exotic mix of citrus and clean, warm male, her senses reeling from his closeness.

'We're married, *cara*. People will expect us to touch each other.'

Her heart skipped like it was trying to break some sort of record. 'I'm not used to people touching me.'

Luca brushed his bent knuckles against the curve of her cheek, his gaze holding hers in a sensual lock that made her insides quake with desire. 'But you like it when I touch you, *si*?' His thumb moved from her pulse point and stroked along her lower lip. 'You like it very much.'

Artie wanted to deny it but she had hardly helped her case by kissing him back the way she had earlier. Nor was she helping it now by not pulling away from his loose hold. Her willpower had completely deserted her— she wanted his touch, craved it like an addict craved a forbidden substance. She couldn't take her eyes off his mouth, couldn't stop thinking about the warm, sensual pleasure of it moving against hers. Couldn't stop thinking about the stroke and glide of his tongue and how it had sent torrents of need racing through her body.

She drew in a ragged breath and forced her gaze back to his. 'I'm sorry if I keep giving you mixed messages. It wasn't my intention at all.'

He brought her hand up to his mouth and pressed a barely-there kiss to her bent knuckles, his gaze unwavering on hers. 'You're not the only one sending mixed messages.' He dropped her hand and gave a rueful smile. 'I'm not going to change the terms of our marriage. It wouldn't be fair to you.'

Not fair? What was fair about denying her body the fulfilment it craved? 'Are you worried I might fall in love with you?' The question popped out before she could stop it.

His dark eyes dipped to her mouth for a moment, his forehead creasing in a frown as if he was quietly considering the possibility of her developing feelings for him. When his gaze came back to hers it was shuttered. Screened with secret thoughts. 'It would be very foolish of you to do so.' His voice contained a note of gravity that made the hairs on the back of her neck tingle.

'Have you ever been in love with anyone?'

'No.' His answer was fast and flat.

Artie twirled the empty champagne glass in her hand. 'I didn't realise it was possible to prevent oneself from falling in love. From what I've heard it just happens and there's nothing you can do to stop it. Maybe you haven't met the right person yet.'

'I have no doubt such feelings exist between other people but I have no interest in feeling that way about someone.'

'Why?'

Luca shrugged one broad shoulder, his gaze still inscrutable. 'It seems to me an impossible task to be someone's soulmate. To be everything they need and want you to be. I know I can't be that person. I'm too selfish.'

Artie wondered if that was entirely true. He was prepared to marry a virtual stranger to keep his grandfather alive for a few more years. How was that selfish? And he was prepared to hand her back the *castello* at the end of six months instead of keeping his nine-tenths ownership. Hardly the actions of a self-serving man, surely?

Rosa approached at that moment carrying a tray with fresh glasses of champagne. 'Another quick one before the official photos are taken?' she asked with a smile. 'The photographer is setting up near the rose garden.'

Artie put her used glass on the tray and took a new one. *'Grazie.'*

'And you, Signor Ferrantelli?' Rosa turned to Luca, offering him a fresh glass off the tray.

He shook his head. 'Not for me, thanks. One is enough. And please call me Luca.' He took Artie's free hand and nodded in the direction of the photographer. 'Shall we?'

Once a small set of photos were taken, Artie helped Rosa tidy away the refreshments after the priest and photographer had left. But when the housekeeper announced she was going to have an early night, Artie was left at a loose end. She hadn't seen Luca since the photo session—he'd said he wanted to check a few things out on the estate and hadn't yet returned. She'd thought about what he'd said back at the fountain and his reasons for saying it. The more she got to know him, the more she wanted to know. Why was he so adamant about keeping his emotions in check? What was so threatening about loving someone that made him so unwilling to experience it for himself? She might not have any experience when it came to falling in love, but she knew enough from her parents and books and movies it was a real and powerful emotion that was impossible to block once it happened. But since the accident, she had given up on the hope of one day finding true love. Any love she felt would be one-sided, for how could anyone return her love once they knew the destruction she had caused?

Luca had warned her about falling in love with him—*'It would be very foolish of you to do so.'* But how could she stop something that was so beyond her control? She was already aware of her vulnerability where he was concerned. He was so suave and sophisticated, and occupied a world she hadn't been party to her entire adult life. Hadn't his passionate, heart-stopping kiss shown her how at risk she was to developing feelings towards him?

Artie circled her wrist where his fingers had held her. A shiver shimmied down her spine as she recalled the tensile strength in his hand, the springy black masculine hairs that peppered his skin, the way his touch spoke to her flesh, awakening it, enlivening it, enticing it. He was temptation personified and she would be a fool indeed to allow her feelings to get the better of her. He had been clear about the terms of their relationship. Why, then, did she ache for more of his touch? Why, then, did she want to feel his mouth on hers again?

Artie sat in the main salon with her embroidery on her lap, when Luca came in. His hair looked tousled from the wind or the passage of his fingers or both. And he had changed out of his morning suit into jeans and a white cotton shirt, the sleeves rolled back to reveal his strong wrists and forearms. The white shirt highlighted his olive-toned tan, the blue jeans the muscled length of his legs. He brought in with him the fresh smell of outdoors and something else…something that made her female hormones sit up straighter and her senses to go on high alert.

She put the sampler she was working on to one side and crossed one leg over the other, working hard to keep her features neutral. 'I wasn't sure of your plans, so I got Rosa to make up one of the guest rooms for you. It's on the second floor—the green suite over-looking the vineyard.'

His gaze held hers with a watchful intensity. 'So, she knows our marriage is a hands-off affair?'

Artie moistened her lips, conscious of the slow crawl of heat in her cheeks. 'Yes, well, I thought it best. I'm not the best actor when it comes to playing charades, and she's known me a long time and would sense any hint of inauthenticity.'

'I would prefer you not to tell anyone else about the terms of our relationship.' His tone was firm. 'I don't want any idle gossip getting back to my grandfather.'

'Rosa is the soul of discretion. She would never betray a confidence.' It was the one thing Artie could rely on—the housekeeper was loyal and trustworthy to a fault. Rosa had never revealed Artie's struggles to anyone and had always been as supportive as possible.

Luca came over to the sofa where she was sitting and leaned down and picked up the sampler she'd been working on. He ran his fingers over the tiny flower buds and leaves she had embroidered. 'This is exquisite work. Have you been doing it long?' he asked.

Artie shrugged off the compliment but inside she was glowing from his praise. No one apart from her father and Rosa had ever seen her work. 'It's just a hobby. I started doing embroidery after I got out of hospital. I'm self-taught, which you can probably tell.'

He turned the sampler over and inspected

the other side, where the stitches were almost as neat and precise as on the front. 'You undersell yourself, *cara*. You could start a small business doing this sort of thing. Bespoke embroidery. There's a big swing away from factory-produced or sweatshop items. What people want these days is the personal touch.'

'Yes, well, I'm not sure I'm ready for that.' Artie took the sampler out of his hand and folded it and put it inside her embroidery basket, then closed the lid with a definitive movement.

'What's stopping you?'

I'm stopping me.

Her fear of the big, wide world outside the *castello* was stopping her from reaching her potential. She knew it but didn't know how she could do anything to change it. How could she run a business locked away here? She met his probing gaze for a moment before looking away again. The thought of revealing her phobia to him made her blood run cold. What would he think of her? She had effectively married him under false pretences. 'I'm happy leaving it as a hobby, that's all. I don't want to put myself under pressure of deadlines.'

'Speaking of deadlines…' Luca rubbed a

hand down his face, the raspy sound of his palm against his light stubble making her recall how it had felt against her skin when he'd kissed her. 'I'd like to make an early start in the morning. My grandfather gets tired easily, so the first part of the day is better for him to receive visitors.'

Artie blinked. Blinked again. Her pulse began to quicken. Her breathing to shorten. Her skin to tighten. She rose from the sofa on unsteady legs and moved to the bank of windows on the other side of the room. She turned her back to the room and grasped the windowsill with white-knuckled force. 'Maybe you should go alone. I need more time before I—'

'There isn't time to waste.' The intransigent edge to his tone was a chilling reminder of his forceful, goal-directed personality.

Artie swallowed a tight lump in her throat and gripped the windowsill even harder. 'I… I can't go with you.'

There was a beat or two of intense silence. A silence so thick it seemed to be pressing in on her from all four walls and even the ceiling. A silence that echoed in her head and roared in her ears and reminded her she was way out of her depth.

'What do you mean, you can't? We made an agreement, Artie. I expect you to adhere to it.' His voice throbbed with frustration. 'Be ready at seven thirty. I'm not taking no for an answer.'

Artie released her grip on the windowsill and turned to face him. Her stomach was roiling, her skin damp with perspiration, her mind reeling at the thought of going beyond the *castello* gates. 'Luca, please don't do this.' Her voice came out sandpaper-hoarse.

He gave a savage frown. 'Don't do what? All I'm asking is for you to uphold your side of our agreement. Which, I might remind you, is a legal one. You signed the papers my lawyer prepared—remember?'

Artie steepled her hands against her nose and mouth, trying to control her breathing. Her heart was doing cartwheels and star jumps and back flips and her pulse was off the charts. 'It's not that I don't want to go…'

'Then what is it?'

She lowered her hands from her face and pressed her lips together to stop them from trembling. She clasped her hands in front of her body, her fingers tightly interlaced to the point of discomfort. She couldn't bring her gaze up to meet his, so instead aimed it at the carpet near his feet. 'There's something I haven't told you…something important.'

Luca crossed the room until he was standing in front of her. He lifted her chin with the end of his finger and meshed his gaze with hers. His frown was still in place but was more concerned now than angry. 'What?' His tone was disarmingly gentle and his touch on her chin light but strangely soothing. 'Tell me what's going on. I want the truth, *cara*.'

Artie bit the inside of her mouth, trying to find the words to describe her condition. Her weakness. Her shame. 'I… I haven't been outside the *castello* grounds since I was fifteen years old. It's not that I don't want to leave it—I can't.'

His hand fell away from her face, his forehead creased in lines of puzzlement. 'Why can't you? What's stopping you?'

She gave a hollow, self-deprecating laugh and pointed a finger at her chest. '*I'm* stopping me.' She stepped back from him and wrapped her arms around her body. 'I have crippling social anxiety. I can't cope with crowds and busy, bustling places. I literally freeze or have a meltdown—a full-blown panic attack.'

He opened and closed his mouth as if trying to think of something to say.

'I'm sorry,' Artie said. 'I should have told you before now but I was too embarrassed and—'

'Please. Don't apologise.' His voice was husky, his expression etched with concern. He shook his head like he was trying to get his muddled thoughts in some sort of order. 'Why didn't your father say something to me? He led me to believe you were—'

'Normal?' She raised her brows in an arch manner. 'Is that the word you were looking for? I'm hardly that, am I?'

Luca made a rough sound at the back of his throat. '*Cara*, please don't run yourself down like that. Have you seen a health professional about it?'

'Four.'

'And?'

Artie spread her hands outwards. 'And nothing. I couldn't cope with the side effects of medication. Meditation and mindfulness helped initially but not enough to get me outside the *castello* grounds. Talk therapy helped too at first but it was expensive and I didn't have the time with my caring responsibilities with Papa to keep going with it.' She gave a sigh and added, 'I found it exhausting, to be honest. Talking about stuff I didn't really want to talk about.'

'The accident?'

Artie nodded, her gaze slipping out of reach of his. 'So, there you have it. My life in a nutshell—no pun intended.'

Luca brushed a finger down her cheek. 'Look at me, *cara*.' It was a command but so gently delivered it made something move inside her chest like the slow flow of warm honey.

Artie raised her eyes back to his, the tip of her tongue sneaking out to sweep over her lips. 'I'm sorry for misleading you. You probably wouldn't have married me if you'd known. But I was so desperate to keep the *castello*. I don't know what I'd do without it. It's the only home I've ever known and if I'm forced to leave...' She bit her lip until she winced. 'I can't leave. I just can't.'

He touched her lip with the pad of his thumb. 'Stop doing that. You'll make it bleed.' His tone was gruff and gently reproving, his gaze surprisingly tender. 'We'll find a way to manage this.'

'How? If your grandfather is too ill to travel, then how will I ever get to meet him?'

'Technology to the rescue.' He gave a quick smile and patted his jeans pocket, where his phone was housed. 'We can set up a video call. Nonno's eyesight isn't great and he's not keen on mobile phones but it will be better than nothing.'

Artie moved a step or two away, her arms crossing over her body, her hands rubbing up and down her upper arms as if warding off a chill. 'You're being very understanding about this... I wouldn't blame you if you tore up the agreement and took full possession of the *castello*.'

Please God, don't let him do that. Please. Please. Please.

Luca came up behind her and placed his hands on her shoulders. 'That's not going to happen.' She suppressed a shiver as the movement of air when he spoke disturbed the loose strands of her hair around her neck. 'We'll work together to solve this.'

Artie turned to face him with a frown. 'Why are you being so generous? You said earlier today you're a selfish man, but I'm not seeing it.'

His smile was lopsided and his hands gently squeezed the tops of her shoulders. 'I can be extremely selfish when it comes to getting what I want.' His gaze drifted to her mouth and her heart skipped a beat. After a moment, his eyes came back to hers. Dark. Lustrous. Intense. The air suddenly vibrating with crackling energy as if all the oxygen particles had been disturbed.

'Luca?' Her voice was barely audible, whisper-soft. Her hand crept up to touch his lean jaw, her fingers trailing over the light prickle of his stubble. She sent her index finger around the firm contours of his mouth, the top lip and then the slightly fuller lower one. He drew in a sharp breath as if her touch excited him, thrilled him, tempted him.

His hand came up and his fingers wrapped around her slim wrist as if to pull her hand from his face. But then he made a low, deep sound at the back of his throat and his head came down and his mouth set fire to hers.

CHAPTER SIX

LUCA KNEW HE should stop the kiss before it got out of control. Knew he shouldn't draw her closer to his body where his blood was swelling him fit to burst. Knew he was forty times a fool to be tempted to change the rules on their paper marriage. But right then, all he could do was explore her soft mouth and let his senses run wild with the sweet, tempting taste of her lips. She opened to him on a breathless sigh and the base of his spine tingled when her tongue met his—shy and yet playful, innocent and yet daring. Need drove him to kiss her more deeply, to hold her more closely, to forget about the restrictions he'd placed on their relationship. Call him reckless, call him foolish, but right now he would die without the sweet temptation of her mouth responding to his.

Artie pressed herself against him, her arms

winding around his neck, her young, slim body fitting against him as if fashioned specially for him. He ached to explore the soft perfection of her breasts, to glide his hands over her skin, to breathe in the scent of her, to taste her in the most intimate way possible.

His hands settled on her hips, holding her to the aching throb in his pelvis, his conscience at war with his body. He finally managed to find the willpower to drag his mouth off hers, but he couldn't quite bring himself to let her go.

'You know this can't happen.' His voice was so rough it sounded like he'd swallowed ground glass.

She looked up at him with eyes bright and shining with arousal. 'Why can't it? We're both consenting adults.'

Luca placed his hands around her wrists and pulled her arms from around his neck, but he still didn't release her. His fingers circled her wrists in a loose hold, his desire for her chomping at the bit like a bolting thoroughbred stallion. 'You know why.'

Her mouth tightened, her cheeks pooling with twin circles of pink. 'Because I'm a virgin? Is that it?'

Luca released her wrists and stepped away,

dragging a hand through his hair in an effort to get his pulse rate to go back to somewhere near normal. 'It's not just about that.'

'Are you saying you don't find me attractive? Not desirable?' Self-doubt quavered in her tone.

Luca let out a gusty sigh. 'I find you extremely attractive and desirable but that's not why I married you. It's not part of the deal. It will make things too complicated when we end it.'

'How do you know that? People have flings all the time without falling in love with each other. Why not us?'

Luca put some distance between their bodies, but even a metre or so away he could still feel the magnetic pull of hers. 'You're young, Artie. Not just in chronological years but in experience. You said it yourself—you haven't been outside the *castello* for ten years. Those were ten valuable growing-up years.'

Her expression soured and hurt coloured her tone. 'You think I'm immature. A child in an adult's body? Is that what you're saying?'

Luca pressed his lips together, fighting to keep his self-control in check. Her adult body was temptation personified but he had to keep his hands off her. It wouldn't be fair to take things to another level, not now he knew how limited her experience. He was the first man to kiss her, to touch her, to expose her to male desire. She was like a teenager experiencing her first crush. A physical crush that had to stop before it got started. 'I'm saying I'm not the right man for you.'

'Consider my offer withdrawn.' She folded her arms around her body and sent him a sideways glance. 'Sorry if I offended you by being so brazen. Believe me, I surprised myself. I don't know what came over me.'

Luca fought back a wry smile. 'We should keep kissing to the absolute minimum.'

Artie gave an indifferent shrug but her eyes displayed her disappointment. 'Fine by me.'

The silence throbbed with a dangerous energy. An energy Luca could feel in every cell of his body. Humming, thrumming sensual energy, awakened, stirred, unsatisfied.

It would be so easy to take back everything he had said and gather her in his arms, to assuage the longing that burned in his body with hot, flicking tongues of flame, to teach her the wonder of sexual compatibility—for he was sure they would be compatible.

He had not felt such electrifying chemistry from kissing someone before. He had not felt such a rush of lust from holding someone close to his body. He had not felt so dangerously tempted to throw caution to the wind and sink his body into the soft silk of another's.

Artie released her arms from around her middle and absently toyed with her wedding ring. 'If you don't mind, I think I'll go to bed.' Her cheeks reddened and she hastily added, 'Alone, I mean. I wasn't suggesting you join—'

'Goodnight, *cara.*'

Artie bolted up the stairs as if she were being chased by a ghost. *Eek.* How could she have been so gauche as to practically beg Luca to make love to her? She couldn't understand why she had been so wanton in her behaviour. Was there something wrong with her? Had her lack of socialising with people her own age affected her development? Her body had woken from a long sleep the moment he kissed her at the wedding. His mouth had sent shivers of longing to every pore of her skin, made her aware of her female needs and desires, made her hungry for a deeper, more powerful connection. A physical connection that would ease the tight, dragging ache in her core.

She closed her bedroom door behind her, letting out a ragged breath. *Fool. Fool. Fool.* He had laid down the rules—a paper marriage with no emotional attachment. A business contract that was convenient and for both parties. But what was convenient about the way she felt about Luca? The heat and fire of his touch made her greedy for more. She had felt his physical response to her, so why was he denying them both the pleasure they both craved?

Because he doesn't want you to fall in love with him.

Artie walked over to her bed and sank onto the mattress with another sigh. Luca thought her too young and innocent for him, too inexperienced in the ways of the world for their relationship to be on an equal footing. But the way her body responded to him made her feel more than his equal. It made her feel alive and feminine and powerful in a way she had never imagined she could feel.

She looked down at the engagement and wedding rings on her left hand, the symbol of their union as a married couple. She was tied to him by law but not by love. And she was fine with that. Mostly. What she wanted was to be tied to him in desire, to explore the electrifying chemistry between them, to indulge herself in the world of heady sensuality.

Artie bounced off the bed and went to her bathroom, staring at her reflection in the mirror above the marble basin. Her eyes were overly bright, her lips still pink and swollen from Luca's passionate kiss. She touched her lower lip with her fingers, amazed at how sensitive it was, as if his kiss had released every one of her nerve endings from a deep freeze.

Artie touched a hand to the ache in the middle of her chest. So, this was what rejection felt like. The humiliation of wanting someone who didn't want you back.

Why am I so unlucky in the lottery of life?

Luca wasn't a drinker, but right then he wanted to down a bottle of Scotch and throw the empty bottle at the wall. He wanted to stride upstairs to Artie's bedroom and take her in his arms and show her how much he wanted her. He wanted to breathe in the scent of her skin, taste the sweet nectar of her lips, glide his hands over her beautiful body and take them both to paradise. But the hard lessons learned from his father's and brother's death had made him super-cautious when it came to doing things that couldn't be undone.

Making love with Artie would change everything about their relationship. It would change the dynamic between them, pitching them into new territory, dangerous territory that clashed with his six-month time limit.

He had thought himself a good judge of character, someone who didn't miss important details. And yet he hadn't picked up on Artie's social phobia, but it all made perfect sense now. Why she hadn't been at the hospital when he'd visited her father. Why she'd insisted on the wedding being held at the *castello* instead of at one of the local churches. Why she had such a guarded air about her, closed off almost, as if she was uncomfortable around people she didn't know. He still couldn't get his head around the fact that she had spent ten years living almost in isolation. Ten years! It was unthinkable to someone like him, who was rarely in the same city two nights in a row. He lived out of hotels rather than at his villa in Tuscany. He lived in the fast lane because slowing down made him think too much, ruminate too much, hurt too much.

It was easier to block it out with work.

Work was his panacea for all ills. He had built his father's business into a behemoth of success. He had brokered deals all over the world and cashed in on every one of them. Big time. He had more money than he knew what to do with. It didn't buy him happiness but it did buy him freedom. Freedom from the ties that bound others into dead-end jobs, going-nowhere relationships and the drudgery of duty-bound responsibilities.

Luca walked over to the windows of his suite at the *castello*. The moon was full and cast the *castello* grounds in an ethereal light. The centuries-old trees, the gnarled vines, the rambling roses were testament to how many generations of Artie's family had lived and loved here.

Love. The trickiest of emotions. The one he avoided, because loving people and then letting them down was soul destroying. The stuff of nightmares, a living torture he could do without.

Luca watched as a barn owl flew past the window on silent wings. Nature going about its business under the cloak of moonlight. The *castello* could be restored into a showcase of antiquity. The gardens tended to and nurtured back into their former glory, the ancient vines grafted and replanted to produce award-winning wine. It would cost money... lots of money—money Artie clearly didn't have. But it would be his gift to her for the time she had given up to be married to him.

Six months, and day one was just about over. A day when he had discovered his bride was an introverted social phobic who had never been kissed until his mouth touched hers. A young woman who had not socialised with her peers outside the walls of the *castello*. A young woman who was still a virgin at the age of twenty-five. A modern-day Sleeping Beauty who had yet to be woken to the pleasures of sex.

Stop thinking about sex.

But how could he when the taste of her mouth was still on his lips? The feel of her body pressed against him was branded on his flesh. The ache of desire still hot and tight and heavy in his groin.

The *castello* was huge, and Artie's bedroom was a long, wide corridor away from his, but his awareness of her had never been more heightened and his self-control never more tested. What was it about her that made him so tempted to throw his rules to one side?

Her unworldly youth? Her innocence? Her sensual allure? It was all those things and more besides. Things he couldn't quite name but he was aware of them all the same. He felt it in his body when he kissed her. A sense of rightness, as if every kiss he'd experienced before had been erased from his memory so that her mouth could be the new benchmark of what a kiss should be. He felt it when he touched her face and the creamy perfection of her skin made his fingers tingle in a way they had never done when touching anyone else. He felt it when he held her close to his body, the sense that her body was a perfect match for his.

Luca turned away from the window with a sigh of frustration. He needed his laptop so he could immerse himself in work but he'd left it in the car. He knew there wouldn't be too many bridegrooms tapping away on their laptops on their wedding night, but he was not a normal bridegroom.

And he needed to keep reminding his body of that too.

When Artie came downstairs the following morning, Rosa was laying out breakfast in the morning room, but not with her usual energy and vigour. Her face was pale and there were lines of tiredness around her eyes.

'Are you okay?' Artie asked, going to her.

Rosa put a hand to her forehead and winced. 'I have the most dreadful headache.'

'Then you must go straight back to bed. I'll call the doctor and—'

'No, I'll be fine. It's just a headache. I've had them before.'

Artie frowned at the housekeeper's pallor and bloodshot eyes. 'You don't look at all well. I insist you go upstairs to bed. I'll manage things down here. It's about time you had some time to yourself. You've been going non-stop since Papa died. And well before that too.' Artie didn't like admitting how dependent she had become on the housekeeper but she wouldn't have been able to cope without Rosa running errands for her.

Rosa began to untie her apron, her expression etched with uncertainty. 'Are you sure?'

Artie took the apron from the housekeeper and tossed it to one side. 'Upstairs. Now. I'll check on you in a couple of hours. And if you're not feeling better by then, I'm calling the doctor.'

'*Sì, sì*, Signora Ferrantelli.' Rosa mock-saluted Artie and then she left the room.

Artie released a sigh and pulled out a chair to sit down at the breakfast table but her appetite had completely deserted her. What *would* she do without Rosa? The housekeeper was her link to the outside world. Her only true friend. If anything happened to Rosa she would be even more isolated.

Stranded.

But you have a husband now...

The sound of firm footsteps approaching sent a tingle down Artie's spine. She swivelled in her chair to see Luca enter the breakfast room. His hair was still damp from a shower, his face cleanly shaven, the sharp tang of his citrus-based aftershave teasing her nostrils. He was wearing blue jeans and a white T-shirt that lovingly hugged his muscular chest and ridged abdomen.

'Good morning.' Her tone was betrayingly breathless and her cheeks grew warm. 'Did you sleep well?'

'Morning.' He pulled out the chair opposite, sat down and spread his napkin over his lap. 'I ran into Rosa when I was coming down. She didn't look well.'

Artie picked up the jug of fresh orange juice and poured some into her glass. 'I've sent her back to bed. She's got a bad headache. She gets them occasionally.' She offered him the juice but he shook his head and reached for the coffee pot. The rich aroma of freshly brewed coffee filled the air.

Luca picked up his cup, glancing at her over the rim. 'Has she got plans to retire? This is a big place to take care of. Does anyone come in to help her?'

Artie chewed at the side of her mouth. 'They used to but we had to cut back the staff a while back. I help her. I enjoy it, actually. It's a way of thanking her for helping me all these years.'

'And how does she help you?' His gaze was unwavering, almost interrogating in its intensity.

Artie lowered her gaze and stared at the beads of condensation on her glass of orange juice. 'Rosa runs errands for me. She picks up shopping for me, the stuff I can't get online, I mean. She's been with my family for a long time. This is her home. Here, with me.'

Luca put down his cup with a clatter on the saucer. 'She can't stay here for ever, Artie. And neither can you.' His tone was gentle but firm, speaking a truth she recognised but didn't want to face.

She pushed back her chair and tossed her

napkin on the table. 'Will you excuse me? I want to check on Rosa.'

'Sit down, *cara*.' There was a thread of steel underlining each word. The same steel glinting in his eyes and in the uncompromising line of his jaw.

Artie toyed with the idea of defying him, a secret thrill shooting through her at the thought of what he might do to stop her flouncing out of the room. Grasp her by the wrists? Hold her to his tempting body? Bring that firm mouth down on hers in another toe-curlingly passionate kiss? She held his gaze for a heart-stopping moment, her pulse picking up its pace, the backs of her knees fizzing. But then she sat heavily in the chair, whipped her napkin across her lap and threw him a look so sour it could have curdled the milk in the jug. 'I hope you're not going to make a habit of ordering me about like I'm some sort of submissive slave.'

His eyes continued to hold hers in a battle of wills. 'I want to talk to you about your relationship with Rosa. I get that she's been supportive for a long time and you see her as a friend you can rely on, but what if she's actually holding you back from developing more autonomy?'

Artie curled her lip. 'I didn't know you had a psychology degree amongst your other impressive achievements.'

'I don't need a psychology degree to see what's happening here.' He picked up a teaspoon and stirred his coffee even though he didn't take sugar or milk. He put the teaspoon down again and continued. 'I know it's hard for you but—'

'How do you know anything of what it's like for me?' She banged her hand on the table, rattling the cups and saucers. 'You're not me. You don't live in my mind, in my body. I'm the only one who knows what this is like for me.' Her chest was tightening, her breathing becoming laboured, her skin breaking out in a sweat. She could feel the pressure building. The fear climbing up her spine. The dread roiling in her stomach. The hammering of her heart. The panic spreading, growing, expanding, threatening to explode inside her head.

Luca rose from his seat and came around to her side of the table and crouched down beside her chair. He took one of her hands in his, enclosing it within the warm shelter of his. 'Breathe, *cara*. Take a slow, deep breath and let it out on the count of three. One. Two. Three. And again. That's it. Nice and slow.'

Artie concentrated on her breathing, holding tightly to the solid anchor of his hand, drawing comfort from his deep and calming tone. The panic gradually subsided, retreating like a wild beast that had been temporarily subdued by a much bigger, stronger opponent. After a long moment, she let out a rattling sigh. 'I'm okay now… I think…' She tried to remove her hand but he kept a firm but gentle hold on her, stroking the back of her hand with his thumb in slow, soothing strokes that made every overwrought cell in her body quieten.

'Take your time, *mia piccola*.'

Artie chanced a glance at his concerned gaze. 'I suppose you think I'm crazy. A mad person who can't walk out of her own front gate.'

Luca placed his other hand beneath her chin and locked her gaze on his. His eyes were darkened by his wide pupils, the green and brown flecks in his irises reminding her of a nature-themed mosaic. 'I don't think any such thing.' He gave a rueful twist of his mouth and continued. 'When my father and brother drowned, I didn't leave the house for a month after their funeral.' A shadow passed across his face like scudding grey clouds. 'I couldn't face the real world without them in it. It was a terrible time.' His tone was weighted with gravitas, his expression drawn in lines of deep sadness.

Artie squeezed his hand. 'It must have been so tragic for you and your mother. How did you survive such awful loss?'

One side of his mouth came up in a smile that wasn't quite a smile. 'There are different types of survival, *si*? I chose to concentrate on forging my way through the morass of grief by studying hard, acing my exams and taking over my father's company. I taught myself not to think about my father and brother. Nothing could bring them back, but I figured I could make my father proud by taking up the reins of his business even though it was never my aspiration to do so. That was my brother's dream.' His half-smile faded and the shadow was back in his gaze.

Artie ached for what he had been through, knowing first-hand how such tragic loss impacted on a person. The way it hit you at odd moments like a sudden stab, doubling you over with unbearable pain. The ongoing reminders—birthdays, anniversaries, Christmas, Mother's Day. So many days of the year when it was impossible to forget. And then there was the guilt that never went away. It hovered over her every single day of her life. 'How did your mother cope with her grief?'

Luca released her hand and straightened to his full height. Artie could sense him withdrawing into himself as if the mention of his mother pained him more than he wanted to admit. 'Enough miserable talk for now. Finish your breakfast, *cara*. And after that, we will call my grandfather and I'll introduce you to him.'

Her stomach fluttered with nerves. 'What if he doesn't accept me? What if he doesn't like me or think I'm suitable?'

Luca stroked his hand over the top of her head, his expression inscrutable. 'Don't worry. He will adore you the minute he meets you.'

CHAPTER SEVEN

LUCA CALLED HIS GRANDFATHER on his phone a short time later and selected the video-call option. He sat with Artie on the sofa in the salon and draped an arm around her waist to keep her in the range of the camera. The fragrance of her perfume wafted around his nostrils, her curly hair tickling his jaw when she leaned closer. His grandfather's image came up on the screen and Luca felt Artie tense beside him. He gave her a gentle squeeze and smiled at her before turning back to face his grandfather.

'Nonno, allow me to introduce you to my beautiful wife Artemisia—Artie for short. We were married yesterday.'

The old man frowned. 'Your wife? *Pah!* You think I'm a doddering old fool or something? You said you were never getting married and now you present me with a wife?

Why didn't you bring her here to meet me in person?'

'We're on our honeymoon, Nonno,' Luca said, wishing, not for the first time, it was true. 'But soon, *sì?*'

'*Buongiorno*, Signor Ferrantelli,' Artie said. 'I'm sorry you've been ill. It must be so frustrating for you.'

'I'll tell you what's frustrating—having my only grandson gadding about all these years as a freedom-loving playboy, when all I want is to see a great-grandchild before I leave this world. It's his duty, his responsibility to carry on the proud family name by producing a new generation.'

Luca gave a light laugh. 'We've only just got married, Nonno. Give us time.' He suddenly realised he didn't want to share Artie with anyone. He wanted to spend time alone with her, getting to know her better. He wanted her with an ache that wouldn't go away. Ever since he'd kissed her it had smouldered like hot coals inside him. The need to explore her body, to awaken her to the explosive pleasure he knew they would experience together. But he refused to even think about the cosy domestic future his grandfather hoped for him. Babies? A new generation of Ferrantellis? Not going to happen.

'You've wasted so much time already,' Nonno said, scowling. 'Your father was married to your mother and had Angelo and you well before your age.'

'*Sì*, I know.' Luca tried to ignore the dart of pain in his chest at the mention of his father and brother. And his mother, of course. He could barely think of his mother without feeling a tsunami of guilt for how his actions had destroyed her life. Grandchildren might soften the blow for his mother, but how could he allow himself to think about providing them? Family life was something he had never envisaged for himself. How could he when he had effectively destroyed his own family of origin?

'Luca is everything I ever dreamed of in a husband,' Artie piped up in a proud little voice that made something in his chest ping. 'He's definitely worth waiting for.'

Nonno gave a grunt, his frown still in place. 'Did you give her your grandmother's engagement ring?' he asked Luca.

'*Sì*,' Luca said.

Artie lifted her hand to the camera. 'I love it. It's the most gorgeous ring I've ever seen.

I feel incredibly honoured to be wearing it. I wish I could have met your wife. You must miss her terribly.'

'Every day.' Nonno shifted his mouth from side to side, his frown softening its grip on his weathered features. 'Don't leave it too long before you come and see me in person, Artie. I haven't got all the time in the world.'

'You'd have more time if you follow your doctor's advice,' Luca said.

'I'd love to meet you,' Artie said. 'Luca's told me so much about you.'

'Yes, well, he's told me virtually nothing about you,' Nonno said, disapproval ripe in his tone. 'How did you meet?'

'I met Artie through her father,' Luca said. 'I knew she was the one for me as soon as I laid eyes on her.' It wasn't a lie. He had known straight up that Artie was the only young woman his grandfather would approve of as his bride.

Nonno gave another grunt. 'Let's hope you can handle him, Artie. He's a Ferrantelli. We are not easy to live with but if you love him it will certainly help.'

'I think he's the most amazing man I've ever met,' Artie said, softly. 'Take care of yourself, Signor Ferrantelli. I hope to meet you in person soon.'

The most amazing man she'd ever met? Luca mentally laughed off the compliment. Artie had met so few men it wasn't hard to impress her. What he wanted to do was help her get over her phobia. Not just because he wanted her to meet his grandfather but because he knew it would open up opportunities and experiences for her that had been denied her for way too long. But would she trust him enough to guide her through what would no doubt be a difficult and frightening journey for her?

Artie turned to face Luca once the call had ended. His arm was still around her waist and every nerve beneath her skin was acutely aware of its solid warm presence. 'I'm not so sure we convinced him. Are you?'

Luca's expression was etched in frowning lines. 'Who knows?' His features relaxed slightly and he added, 'You did well. That was a nice touch about me being your dream husband. It's kind of scary how convincing you sounded.' He brushed a stray strand of hair away from her face, his gaze darkening.

Artie disguised a swallow, her heart giving a little kick when his eyes drifted to her mouth. 'Yes, well, I surprised myself, actually.' She frowned and glanced down at the engagement and wedding rings on her hand and then lifted her gaze back to his. 'I feel like I'm letting you down by not being able to leave the *castello*. If we'd gone in person to see him, or even better, married somewhere closer so your grandfather could have attended…'

'You're not letting me down at all,' Luca said. 'But what if I tried to help you? We could start small and see how it goes—baby steps.'

'I've had help before and it hasn't worked.'

'But you haven't had my help.' He smiled and took her hand, running his thumb over the back of it in gentle strokes. 'It's worth a try, surely?'

Panic crawled up her spine and sent icicles tiptoeing across her scalp. 'What, now?'

'No time like the present.'

Artie compressed her lips, trying to control her breathing. 'I don't know…'

He raised her chin with the end of his finger. 'Trust me, *cara*. I won't push you further than you can manage. We will take it one step at a time.'

Artie swallowed and then let out a long, ragged breath. 'Okay. I'll try but don't be mad at me if I don't get very far.'

He leaned down and pressed a light kiss to the middle of her forehead. 'I won't get mad at you, *mia piccola*. I'm a very patient man.'

A few minutes later, Artie stood with Luca on the front steps of the *castello*, her gaze focussed on the long walk to the brass gates in the distance. Her heart was beating so fast she could feel its echo in her ears. Her skin was already damp with perspiration, and her legs trembling like a newborn foal's. She desperately wanted to conquer her fear, now more than ever. She wanted to meet Luca's grandfather, to uphold her side of their marriage deal but what if she failed yet again? She had failed every single time she had tried to leave the *castello*. It was like a thick glass wall was blocking her exit. She could see the other side to freedom but couldn't bring herself to step over the boundary lines. The *castello* was safe. She was safe here. Other people on the outside were safe from *her*.

What would happen if she went past her self-imposed boundary?

Luca took her hand and smiled down at

her. 'Ready? One step at a time. Take all the time you need.'

Artie sucked in a deep breath and went down the steps to the footpath. So far, so good. 'I've done this before, heaps of times, and I always fail.'

'Don't talk yourself into failure, *cara*.' His tone was gently reproving. 'Believe you can do something and you'll do it.'

'Easy for you to say.' Artie flicked him a glance. 'You're confident and run a successful business. You've got runs on the board. What do I have? A big fat nothing.'

Luca stopped and turned her so she was facing him, his hands holding her by the upper arms. 'You have cared for your father for a decade. You quite likely extended his life by doing so. Plus, you're a gifted embroiderer. I have never seen such detailed and beautiful work. You have to start believing in yourself, *cara*. I believe in you.'

Artie glanced past his broad shoulder to the front gates, fear curdling her insides. She let out another stuttering breath and met his gaze once more. 'Okay, let's keep going. I have to do this. I *can* do this.'

'That's my girl,' Luca said, smiling and

taking her by the hand again. 'I'm with you every step of the way.'

Artie took two steps, then three, four, five until she lost count. The gates loomed closer and closer, the outside world and freedom beckoning. But just as she got to about two-thirds of the way down the path a bird suddenly flew up out of the nearby shrubbery and Artie was so startled she lost her footing and would have tripped if Luca hadn't been holding her hand. 'Oh!' she gasped.

'You're okay, it was just a bird.'

Artie glanced at the front gates, her heart still banging against her breastbone. 'I think I'm done for one day.'

He frowned. 'You don't want to try a little more? We're almost there. Just a few more steps.'

She turned back to face the safety of the *castello*, breathing hard. 'I'm sorry but I can't do any more. I'll try again tomorrow.'

And I'll fail just like every other time.

Luca stroked his hand over the back of her head. 'You did well, *mia piccola*.'

Artie gave him a rueful look. 'I failed.'

He stroked her cheek with a lazy finger, his gaze unwavering. 'Failure is when you give up trying.' He took her hand again with another smile. 'Come on. It's thirsty work wrestling demons, *si*?'

Once they were back inside the *castello* in the salon, Artie let out a sigh. 'It's not that I don't want to go outside…'

He handed her a glass of mineral water. 'What are you most frightened of?'

She took the glass from him and set it on the table next to her, carefully avoiding his gaze. 'I'm frightened of hurting people.'

'Why do you think you'll hurt someone?'

Artie lifted her eyes to his. 'It was my fault we had the accident.'

Luca frowned and came over to sit beside her, taking her hands in his. 'But you weren't driving, surely? You were only fifteen, *si*?'

She looked down at their joined hands, her chest feeling so leaden it was almost impossible to take in another breath. 'I wanted to go to a party. My parents didn't want me to go but like teenagers do, I wouldn't take no for an answer. They relented and I went to the party, which wasn't as much fun as I'd hoped. And when my parents picked me up that night…well, my father was tired because it was late and he didn't see the car drifting into his lane in time to take evasive action. I woke up in hospital after being in a coma for a month to find my mother had died instantly and my father was in a wheelchair.'

Luca put his arms around Artie and held her close. 'I'm sorry. I know there are no words to take away the guilt and sadness but you were just a kid.'

Artie eased back to look up at him through blurry vision. 'I haven't ever met anyone else who truly understood.' She twisted her mouth wryly, 'Not that I've met a lot of people in the last ten years.' She lifted her hand to his face and stroked his lean jaw and added. 'But I think you do understand.'

A shadow passed through his gaze and he pulled her hand down from his face. 'You don't know me, *cara*. You don't know what I'm capable of.' His voice contained a note of self-loathing that made the back of her neck prickle.

'Why do you say that?'

He sprang off the sofa in an agitated fashion. 'I haven't told you everything about the day my father and brother died.'

She swallowed tightly. 'Do you want to tell me now?' Her voice came out whisper-soft.

Luca pulled at one side of his mouth with his straight white teeth, his hands planted on his slim hips. Then he released a ragged breath. 'It was my fault they drowned. We were on holiday in Argentina. We had gone to an isolated beach because I'd heard the waves were best there. I wanted to go back in for another surf even though the conditions had changed. I didn't listen to my father. I just raced back in and soon got into trouble.' He winced as if recalling that day caused him immeasurable pain. 'My father came in after me and then my brother. The rip took them both out to sea. I somehow survived. I can never forgive myself for my role in their deaths. I was selfish and reckless, and in trying to save me, they both lost their lives.'

Artie went to him and grasped him by both hands. 'Oh, Luca, you were only a child. Kids do stuff like that all the time, especially teenage boys. You mustn't blame yourself. But I understand how you do…you see, I blame myself for my mother's death and my dad's disability.'

'I do understand.' His eyes were full of pain. 'There were times when I wished I had been the one to die. I'm sure you wished the same. But that doesn't help anyone, does it?'

'No…' She leaned her head against the solid wall of his chest, slipping her arms back around his waist. 'Thank you.'

'For?' The deep, low rumble of his voice reverberated next to her ear.

Artie looked back up at him. 'For listening. For understanding. For not judging.' She took a little hitching breath and added, 'For wanting me when I thought no one ever could.'

Luca brushed his thumb over the fullness of her lower lip, setting off a firestorm in her flesh. 'I want you. I've tried ignoring it, denying it, resisting it, but it won't go away.' His voice dropped to a lower pitch, tortured almost, as if he was fighting a battle within himself between what he should do and what he shouldn't.

Artie licked her lips and encountered the saltiness of his thumb. 'I want you too.' She touched his firm jaw with her hand. 'I don't see why we have to stick to the rules. We are attracted to each other physically. Why not enjoy the opportunity? How else am I going to gain experience? I'm hardly going to meet anyone whilst living here, and we're married anyway, so why not?' She could hardly believe how brave she was being, speaking her needs out loud. But something about Luca made her feel brave and courageous. His desire for her spoke to her on a cellular level, making her aware of her body and its needs in a way she hadn't thought possible.

Luca cupped one side of her face in his hand, his thumb stroking over her cheek in slow, measured strokes. A frown settled between his brows, his eyes darker than she had ever seen them. 'Is that really want you want? A physical relationship, knowing it will end after six months?'

Maybe it won't end.

Artie didn't say it out loud—she was shocked enough at hearing it inside her head.

Since the accident, she had denied herself any dreams of one day finding love, of marrying and having a family. She had destroyed her family, so why should she have one of her own? But now she had met Luca, she realised what she was missing out on. The thrill of being attracted to someone and knowing they desired you back. The perfectly normal needs within her body she had ignored for so long were fully awake and wanting, begging to be assuaged. 'I want to know what it is like to make love with a man,' Artie said. 'I want that man to be you. I trust you to take care of me. To treat me with respect.'

He stroked her hair back from her forehead, his eyes dark and lustrous. 'I can't think of a time when I wanted someone more. But I told myself I wasn't going to take advantage of the situation—of you. I don't think it would be fair to give you false hope that this could lead to anything…more permanent.'

She leaned closer, winding her arms around his neck. 'Stop overthinking it. Do what your heart is telling you, not your head. Make love to me, Luca.'

Luca placed his hands on her hips and bent his head down so their lips were within touching distance. 'Are you sure? There's still time to change your mind.'

Artie pressed her lips against his, once, twice, three times. 'I'm not changing my mind. I want this. I want you.'

He stood and drew her to her feet, dropping a warm, firm kiss to her lips. 'Not here. Upstairs. I want everything to be perfect for you.'

A short time later, they were in Luca's bedroom. He closed the door softly behind them and ran his gaze over Artie. She had expected to feel shy, self-conscious about her body, but as soon as he began to undo the buttons on her top, she shivered with longing, desperate to be naked with him, to feel his skin against her own.

He kissed her lingeringly, taking his time nudging and nibbling her lips, teasing her with his tongue, tantalising her senses with his taste and his touch. His mouth moved down to just below her ear and she shivered as his lips touched her sensitive skin. One of his hands slipped beneath her unbuttoned top, gliding along the skin of her ribcage to cup one of her breasts. His touch was gentle and yet it created a tumultuous storm in her flesh. Her nipple tightened, her breast tingled, her legs weakened as desire shot through her like a missile strike.

'I want to touch you all over.' His tone had a sexy rough edge that made her senses whirl.

'I want to touch you too.' Artie tugged his T-shirt out of his jeans and slid her hands under the fabric to stroke his muscular chest. His warm, hard flesh felt foreign, exotically foreign, unlike anything she had touched before. She explored the hard planes and ridged contours of his hair-roughened chest, marvelling at the difference between their bodies. A difference that excited her, made her crazy with longing, eager to discover more.

Luca unclipped her bra and gazed at her breasts for a long moment, his eyes dark and shining with unmistakable desire. 'So beautiful.' His thumbs rolled over each of her nipples, his gaze intent, as if he found her breasts the most fascinating things he'd ever seen. Before this moment Artie had more or less ignored her breasts other than to do her monthly breast check. But now she was aware of the thousands of nerve-endings that were responding to Luca's touch. Aware of the way her tender flesh tingled and tautened under his touch. Aware of the primal need it triggered in her feminine core—of the ache that longed to feel the hard male presence of his body.

Artie gasped as Luca brought his mouth to her breasts, her hands gripping him by the waist, not trusting her legs to keep her upright as the sensations washed through her. His tongue teased her nipple into a tight point, and then he circled it with a slow sweep of his tongue.

The slight roughness of his tongue against her softer skin evoked another breathless and shuddering gasp from her. 'Oh… *Oh*…'

Luca lifted his mouth off her breast and smiled a bone-melting smile. 'You like that?'

Artie leaned closer, the feel of her naked breasts pressing against his muscular chest sending another riot of tingling sensations through her body. 'I love it when you touch me. I can't get enough of it.'

He slid his hands down to the waistband of her jeans, his fingers warm against her belly as he undid the snap button. Who knew such an action could cause such a torrent of heat in her body? Artie could barely stop her legs from shaking in anticipation. He held her gaze in a sensual lock that made her heart skip and trip. He slid his hand beneath the loosened waistband, cupping her mound through the thin, lacy barrier of her knickers. Her body responded with humid heat, slickening, moistening with the dew of desire.

'I can't seem to get enough of you either,' he said. 'But I don't want to rush you. I want to go slowly to make it good for you.'

Artie placed her hands on the waistband of his jeans. 'Can I?'

His eyes gleamed. 'Go for it.'

She held her breath and undid the fastening and slid down the zipper. She peeled back his underwear and drank in the potent sight of him engorged with blood, thickened with longing. Longing for *her*.

Luca drew in a sharp breath as her fingers skated over his erection. He removed her hand and returned his mouth to hers in a spine-tingling kiss that spoke of the primal need pulsing through his body. The flicker of his tongue against hers, the increasing urgency and pressure of his mouth drew from her a fevered response she hadn't thought possible.

Within a few breathless moments they were both naked and lying on the bed together, Luca's eyes roving over her body in glinting hunger. He placed a hand on her hip, turning her towards him, his expression becoming sober. 'There's something we need to discuss. Protection. We can't let any accidents happen, especially given the terms of our relationship.'

Artie knew he was being reasonable and responsible but a secret part of her flinched at his adamant stance on the six-month time frame. An accidental pregnancy would change everything. It would tie them together for the next eighteen years...possibly for ever. 'I understand. I wouldn't want any...accidents either.' She had not allowed herself to think of one day having a baby but now a vision popped into her head of a gorgeous, dark-haired baby... Luca's baby.

Don't get any ideas. You know the terms. Six months and six months only.

Her conscience had an annoying habit of reminding her of the deal she had made with Luca. A deal she hoped she wouldn't end up regretting in the end.

Luca stroked his hand down the flank of her thigh, his gaze centred on hers. 'It's important to me that you enjoy our lovemaking. I want you to feel comfortable, so please tell me if something isn't working for you or you want to stop at any point.'

Artie traced the shape of his lower lip with her finger. 'I've liked everything so far. I thought I'd be nervous about being naked with someone but this feels completely natural, as if we've done this before in another lifetime. Does that make sense?'

He smiled and captured her hand and pressed a kiss to each of her fingertips, his eyes holding hers. 'In a strange way, yes, although I have to say I've never made love to a virgin before.'

'Are *you* nervous?'

His mouth twisted into a rueful grimace. 'A bit.'

'Don't be.' She pressed her lips to his in a soft kiss. 'I want you to make love to me. I feel like I've been waiting all my life for this moment.'

Luca brought his mouth back to hers in a kiss that drugged her senses and ramped up her desire for him until she was arching her back and whimpering. His hands explored her breasts in soft strokes, his lips and tongue caressing her until she was breathless with longing. The ache between her legs intensified, a hot, throbbing ache that travelled through her pelvis like the spread of fire.

He moved down her body with a series of kisses from her breasts to her belly and then to the heart of her femininity. Artie drew in a breath, tense with excitement as his fingers spread her, his lips and tongue exploring her, teasing a response from her that shook her body into a cataclysmic orgasm. It swept her up in its rolling waves, the pulsations carrying her into a place beyond the reach of thought or even full consciousness. Blissful sensations washed over her, peace flooding her being—the quiet after the storm.

'I had no idea it could be like…like *that*…' Artie could barely get her voice to work and a sudden shyness swept over her.

Luca moved back up her body to plant a kiss to her lips. She could taste herself on his lips and it added a whole new layer of disturbing but delightful intimacy. 'It will only get better.' He brushed his knuckles over her warm cheeks. 'Don't be shy, *cara*.'

Artie bit her lip. 'Easy for you to say. You've probably done this a hundred times, possibly more. I'm a complete novice.'

He smoothed her hair back from her face, his expression suddenly serious. 'The press makes a big thing out of my lifestyle but I haven't been as profligate as they make out. Unfortunately, my grandfather believes what he reads in the press.' His mouth twisted ruefully. 'I've had relationships—fleeting ones that were entirely transactional. And I've always tried not to deliberately hurt anyone. But of course, it still does happen occasionally.'

I hope I don't get hurt.

The potential to get hurt once their relationship came to its inevitable end was a real and present worry, but even so, Artie couldn't bring herself to stop things before they got any more complicated. He had revealed things about himself that made her hungry to learn more about him. His workaholism, his carefully guarded heart, his history of short-term, going-nowhere relationships. He was imprisoned by his lifestyle in the same way she was imprisoned by the *castello*. Would he go back to his playboy existence once they parted?

Artie lifted her hand and stroked his stubbly jaw. 'I want you to make love to me. I want you to experience pleasure too.'

Luca's eyes were dark and hooded as he gazed at her mouth. 'Everything about you brings me pleasure, *cara*. Absolutely everything.' And his mouth came down and sealed hers.

The kiss was long and intense and Artie could feel the tension rising in his body as well as her own. His legs were entangled with hers, his aroused body pressing urgently against her, his breathing as ragged as hers. His mouth moved down to her breasts, subjecting them to a passionate exploration that left her squirming and whimpering with need. She slid her hand down from his chest to his taut abdomen, desperate to explore the hard contours of his body. He drew in a quick breath when her hand encountered his erection and it made her all the bolder in her caresses. He was velvet-wrapped steel, so exotically, erotically different from her, and she couldn't wait to experience those differences inside her body.

Luca eased back and reached for a condom, swiftly applying it before coming back to her, his gaze meshing with hers. 'I'll go slowly but please tell me if you want to stop at any point. I don't want to hurt you.'

Artie brushed his hair back from his forehead, her lower body so aware of his thick male presence at her entrance. 'You won't hurt me.' Her tone was breathless with anticipation, her body aching for his possession.

He gently nudged apart her feminine folds, allowing her time to get used to him as he progressed. Slow, shallow, sensual. Her body welcomed him, wrapping around him without pain, without resistance.

'Are you okay?' he asked, pausing in his movements.

'More than okay.' Artie sighed with pure pleasure, her hands going to his taut buttocks to hold him to her.

He thrust a little deeper, still keeping his movements slow and measured. She arched her hips to take more of him in, her body tingling with darts and arrows of pleasure as his body moved within hers. His breathing rate changed, becoming more laboured as his pace increased. She was swept up into his rhythm, her senses reeling as the tension built to an exquisite crescendo. She was almost at the pinnacle, hovering in the infinitesimal moment before total fulfilment. Wanting, aching, needing to fly but not sure how to do it.

Luca reached down between their bodies and coaxed her swollen feminine flesh into an earth-shattering orgasm. Spirals of intense pleasure burst through her body, ripples and waves and darts of bliss, throwing her senses into a tailspin and her mind into disarray.

Luca reached his release soon after, an agonised groan escaping his lips as his body convulsed and spilled. Artie held him close, breathing in the scent of their lovemaking, thrilled to have brought him to a place of blissful satiation.

Artie lay with him in the peaceful aftermath, her thoughts drifting… The boundaries between the physical and the emotional were becoming increasingly blurred. She knew she would always remember this moment as a pivotal one in her life as a woman.

Luca Ferrantelli. Her husband. Her first lover.

The presence of his body, the desire that drew them together bonded her to him in a way that was beyond the physical. The chemistry between her and Luca was so powerful, so magical it had produced a cataclysmic reaction. An explosion of pleasure she could still feel reverberating throughout her body.

How could she have thought he was arrogant and unyielding? He had taken such respectful care of her every step of the way. He had held back his own release in order to make sure she was satisfied first. She couldn't have asked for a more considerate and generous lover.

But it didn't mean she was falling in love with him.

Artie knew the rules and had accepted them. She could be modern and hip about their arrangement. Sure she could. This was about a physical connection so intense, so rapturous she wanted to make the most of it.

Luca leaned up on one elbow and slowly withdrew from her body, carefully disposing of the condom. He rolled back to cradle one side of her face with his hand, his eyes searching hers. 'How do you feel?' His voice had a husky edge, his expression tender in a way she hadn't been expecting. Had he too been affected by her first time and their first time together?

'I'm fine.'

A frown pulled at his brow. 'I didn't hurt you?'

'Not at all.' She smoothed away his frown

with her fingertip. 'Thanks for being so gentle with me.'

His hand brushed back the hair from her face in the tenderest of movements. 'Your enjoyment is top priority for me. I don't want you to feel you ever have to service my needs above your own.'

Artie ran her fingertip over the fullness of his bottom lip, not quite able to meet his gaze. 'Was it good for you too?'

He tipped up her chin and smiled, and her chest felt like it was cracking open. 'Off the charts.' He leaned down to press a soft, lingering kiss to her lips. He lifted off again, his expression becoming thoughtful. 'I've never been a virgin trophy hunter. A woman's virginity is not something I consider a prize to be claimed or a conquest to be sought.' He captured a loose strand of her hair and tucked it back behind her ear. 'But I have to say I feel privileged to have made love with you.'

Artie wrapped her arms around his waist and leaned her cheek against the wall of his chest. 'I feel privileged too. You made it so special.'

There was a moment or two of silence.

Luca stroked his hand down between

Artie's shoulder blades to the base of her spine. 'I should let you get up and get dressed.'

Artie lifted her head off his chest to smile at him. 'Is that what you really want me to do right now?'

He grinned and pressed her back down on the bed with his weight playfully pinning her. 'Not right now.' And he brought his mouth back down to hers.

CHAPTER EIGHT

LATER THAT MORNING, Luca had to convince himself to get out of bed with Artie. He couldn't remember a time when he had spent a morning more pleasurably. Making love with her for the first time had affected him in a way he hadn't been expecting. The mutual passion they had shared had been beyond anything he had experienced before. And that was deeply troubling.

Why was it so special? Because she was innocent and he so worldly and jaded that making love with her was something completely different from the shallow hook-ups he preferred? Or was it the exquisite feel of her skin next to his? Her mouth beneath his? Her touch, her sighs, her gasps and cries that made him feel more of a man than he ever had before?

The trust she had shown in him had touched

him deeply. And he had honoured that trust by making sure she was completely satisfied, and yet his own satisfaction had risen to a whole new level of experience. It was as if his body had been asleep before now. Operating on a lower setting that didn't fully register all the nuances of mind-blowing sex. The glide of soft hands on his body, the velvet-soft press of lips on his heated skin, the delicious friction of female flesh against him. Every moment was imprinted on his brain, every kiss, every touch branded on his body.

And he wanted it to continue, which was the most troubling thought of all. He, who never stayed with a lover longer than a week or two. He, who never envisaged a future with anyone. He, who had locked down his emotions so long ago he didn't think he had the capacity to feel anything for anyone any more.

And yet...

Every time Artie looked at him with those big brown eyes, something tugged in his chest. Every time her pillow-soft lips met his, fire spread through his body, a raging fire of lust and longing unlike any he had felt before. Every time she smiled it was like encountering sunshine after a lifetime of darkness.

Luca swung his legs over the side of the bed before he was tempted to make love to her for the third time. He turned and held out a hand to her. 'Come on. Time for some more exposure therapy.'

Artie unfolded her limbs and stood in front of him, her hands going to his hips, sending his blood racing. Her eyes were bright and sparkling, her lips swollen from his kisses. 'Let's stay here instead. It'll be more fun.'

Luca gave her a stern look. Exposure therapy was well known to be the pits the first few times but it still had to be endured for results. '*Cara*, you're procrastinating. It's classic avoidance behaviour and it will only make things worse.'

Her gaze lost its playful spark and her mouth tightened. Her hands fell away from his hips and she turned and snatched up a loose bed sheet and covered her nakedness, as if she was suddenly ashamed of her body. 'Last time I looked, you were my temporary husband and lover, not my therapist. I don't appreciate you trying to fix me.'

Luca suppressed a frustrated sigh. 'I'm not trying to fix you, *cara*. I'm trying to help you gain the courage to go a little further each day. I'll be with you all the time and I won't push you into doing anything you don't want to do. You can trust me, okay?'

Her teeth chewed at her lower lip, her gaze still guarded. 'Look, I know you mean well, but we tried it before and I failed.'

'That doesn't mean you'll fail today.'

There was a long moment of silence.

Artie released a long, shuddering breath. 'Okay… I'll give it another try.' She swallowed and glanced at him, her cheeks tinged with pink. 'Do you mind if I have a quick shower first?'

Luca waved his hand towards the bathroom. 'Go right ahead. I'll meet you downstairs in half an hour.' He needed to put some space between them before he was tempted to join her in the shower.

She walked to the door of the bathroom, then stopped and turned to look back at him with a frown between her eyes. 'Did you only make love to me to make me more amenable to going outside the *castello* grounds with you?'

'I made love with you because I wanted you and you wanted me.'

And I still want you. Badly.

Her teeth did another nibble of her lip, uncertainty etched on her features. 'I hope I don't disappoint you this time…'

Luca came over to her and tipped up her chin and planted a soft kiss to her lips. 'You could never disappoint me.'

Artie showered and changed with her mind reeling at what Luca wanted her to do. She had failed so many times. Why should this time be any different? Panic flapped its wings in her brain and her belly, fear chilled her skin and sent a tremble through her legs. But she took comfort in the fact he promised to stay with her, to support her as she confronted her fear—a fear she had lived with so long it was a part of her identity. She literally didn't know who she was now without it. But making love with Luca had given her the confidence to step outside her comfort zone. Her skin still sang with the magic of his touch, the slightly tender muscles in her core reminding her of the power and potency of his body.

Luca was waiting for her downstairs and took her hand at the front door. 'Ready? Our goal is to go farther than we went yesterday— even if we don't make it outside the gates it will still be an improvement. That's the way to approach difficult tasks—break them up into smaller, achievable segments.'

Artie drew in a shaky breath, her chest feeling as if a flock of frightened finches were trapped inside. 'Sounds like a sensible plan. Okay, let's give it a go.'

The sun was shining and white fluffy clouds were scudding across the sky. A light breeze scented with old-world roses danced past Artie's face. Luca's fingers wrapped around hers, strong, warm, supportive, and she glanced up at him and gave a wobbly smile. 'Thanks for being so patient.'

He looped her arm through his, holding her close as they walked slowly but surely down the cobbled footpath to the wrought-iron front gates. 'I probably made you go too fast the first time. Let's slow it down a bit. We've got plenty of time to stop and smell the roses.'

Artie walked beside him and tried to concentrate on the spicy fragrance of the roses rather than the fear crawling over her skin. She was conscious of Luca's muscular arm linked with hers and the way he matched his stride to hers. She flicked him another self-conscious glance. 'You must think this is completely ridiculous. That *I'm* completely ridiculous.'

He gave her a light squeeze. 'I don't think that at all. Fear is a very powerful emotion. It can be paralysing. Fear of failure, fear of success, fear of—'

'Commitment,' Artie offered.

There was a slight pause before he answered. 'That too.'

'Fear of love.' She was on a roll, hardly noticing how many cobblestones there were to go to the front gate.

There was another silence, longer this time, punctured only by the sound of the whispering breeze and twittering birds in the overgrown shrubbery.

'Fear of not being capable of loving.' His tone contained a rueful note.

Artie stopped walking to look up at his mask-like expression. 'Why do you think you're not capable of loving someone? You love your grandfather, don't you?'

Luca gave a twisted smile that didn't quite reach his eyes. 'Familial love is an entirely different sort of love. However, choosing to love someone for the rest of my life is not something I feel capable of doing. I would only end up hurting them by letting them down in the end.'

'But is loving someone a choice?' Artie

asked. 'I mean, I haven't fallen in love myself but I've always understood it to be outside of one's control. It just happens.'

He captured a loose tendril of her hair and tucked it back behind her ear. His touch was light and yet electrifying, his gaze dark and inscrutable. 'A lucky few find love for a lifetime. But some lives are tragically cut short and then that same love becomes a torture for the one left behind.'

'Is that what happened to your mother?'

Luca's gaze drifted into the distance, his expression becoming shadowed. 'I will never forget the look of utter devastation on my mother's face when she was told my father and brother had drowned. She didn't come with us that day and when only I came home...' He swallowed tightly and continued in a tone rough and husky with banked-down emotion. 'For months, years, she couldn't look at me without crying. I found it easier to keep my distance. I hated seeing her like that, knowing I was responsible for what happened.'

Artie wrapped her arms around his waist and hugged him. 'Oh, Luca, you have to learn to forgive yourself. I'm sure your mother doesn't blame you. You were a young teenager. She was probably relieved you hadn't been taken as well. It could have happened. You could have all been drowned.'

He eased out of her hug and gave her a grim look. 'There were times in the early days when I wished I had been taken with them. But then I realised I owed it to my father and brother to live the best life I could to honour them.'

A life of hard work. A life with no love. No commitment. No emotional vulnerability. A life of isolation...not unlike her own.

A life of isolation she would go back to once their marriage was over.

Artie glanced at the front gates of the *castello* and drew in a shuddering breath. The verdigris-covered gates blurred in front of her into a grotesque vision of blue and green twisted metal. The sun disappeared behind a cloud and the birds suddenly went quiet as if disturbed by a menacing predator lurking in the shadows.

'Luca, I don't think I can go any further...'

He took her hand and looped her arm through his once more. 'You'll be fine. We're almost there. We've gone farther than yesterday. Just a few more steps and we'll be—'

'No.' Artie pulled out of his hold and took

a few stumbling steps back towards the *castello*. 'I can't.'

Luca captured her by the wrist and brought her back to face him, his expression concerned. 'Whoa there. Slow down or you'll trip and twist your ankle.'

Her chest was so restricted she couldn't take a breath. Her stomach was churning, her knees shaking, her skin breaking out in a clammy sweat. She closed her eyes and a school of silverfish swam behind her eyelids. She opened her eyes but she couldn't see past the sting of tears. She tried to gulp in a breath but her throat wouldn't open enough for it to get through.

I'm going to die. I'm going to die. I'm going to die.

The words raced through her mind as if they were being chased by the formless fear that consumed her.

Luca gathered her close to his chest and stroked her stiff back and shoulders with slow, soothing strokes. 'Breathe, *cara*. Take a deep breath and let it out on the count of three. One. Two. Three. And again. One. Two. Three. Keep going, *mia piccola*. One. Two. Three.'

His gently chanted words and the stroke

of his hands began to quieten the storm inside her body. The fog in Artie's brain slowly lifted, the fear gradually subsiding as the oxygen returned to her bloodstream.

She was aware of every point of contact with his body—her breasts pressed against his chest, the weight of his arm around her back, his other hand moving up and down between her shoulder blades in those wonderfully soothing strokes, his pelvis warm and unmistakably male against hers, his chin resting on the top of her head. She was aware of the steady *thud, thud, thud* of his heart against her chest, the intoxicating smell of his skin, the need awakening anew in her body. Pulses, contractions, flickers and tingles deep in her core.

Luca lifted his chin off her head and held her slightly aloft, his gaze tender. 'You did well—it's only our second try. Don't feel bad you didn't make it all the way. We'll try again tomorrow.'

Artie chewed her lip, ashamed she hadn't gone further. 'What if I'm never able to do it? What if I—?'

His finger pressed softly down on her lips to silence her self-destruction beliefs. 'Don't talk yourself into failure, *cara*. I know you can do it. You want to get better and that's half the battle, is it not?'

Artie gave a tremulous smile, heartened by his belief in her. Comforted by his commitment to helping her. Touched by his concern and patience and support. 'I do want to get better. I'm tired of living like this. I want to experience life outside the walls of the *castello*.'

He cupped one side of her face in his hand. 'And I can't wait to show you life outside these walls. There are so many things we can do together—dinner, dancing, sightseeing, skiing, trekking. I will enjoy showing you all my favourite places.'

Artie gave a self-deprecating smile. 'I have a lot of catching up to do. And only six months in which to do it.'

Luca's hand fell away from her face, his expression tightening as if her mentioning the time limit on their relationship was jarring to him. 'Of course, the most important thing we need to do is introduce you to my grandfather. I can't use the excuse of being on honeymoon for weeks or months on end.'

'Maybe he'll be well enough to come here soon.' It was a lame hope but she articulated it anyway.

His hand scraped back his hair in a distracted manner. 'There's no guarantee that's going to happen. Besides, I have work to see to. I can't stay here indefinitely.'

'I'm not stopping you from doing your work,' Artie said. 'You can leave any time you like.'

His gaze met hers. Strong. Determined. Intractable. 'I want you with me.'

A frisson scooted down her spine at the dark glint in his eyes. The glint that spoke of the desire still smouldering inside him—the same desire smouldering inside her. She could feel the crackle of their chemistry in the air. Invisible currents of electricity that zapped and fizzed each time their eyes met and each time they touched. He stepped closer and slid his hand beneath the curtain of her hair, making her skin tingle and her blood race. His gaze lowered to her mouth, the sound of his breath hitching sending another shiver cascading down her spine.

'I didn't think it was possible that I could want someone so much.' His tone was rough around the edges.

Artie moved closer, her hands resting on the hard wall of his chest, her hips clamped to his, heat pooling in her core. 'I want you too.'

He rested his forehead on hers, their breath mingling in the space between their mouths. 'It's too soon for you. You'll be sore.' His voice was low, his hands resting on her hips.

Artie brought her mouth closer to his, pressing a soft kiss to his lips. 'I'm not sore at all. You were so gentle with me.'

He groaned and drew her closer, his mouth coming down on hers in a kiss that spoke of banked-down longing. She opened to the commanding thrust of his tongue, her senses whirling as he called her tongue into sensual play. Need fired through her body, hot streaks of need that left no part of her unaffected. Tingles shot down her spine and through her pelvis, heating her to boiling point. Her intimate muscles responded with flickers and fizzes of delight, her bones all but melting. One of his hands moved from her hip to cup her breast through her clothes, sending another fiery tingle through her body.

He deepened the kiss even further, his hand going beneath her top and bra to cup her skin on skin. The warmth of his palm and the possessive weight of his fingers sent her pulse soaring. He stroked her nipple into a tight bud of exquisite sensations, powerful sensations for such a small area of her body. He lifted his mouth off hers and lowered his lips to her breast, his tongue swirling over her engorged nipple, his teeth gently tugging and releasing in a passionate onslaught that made her gasp with delight.

The sound of Luca's phone ringing from inside his trouser pocket evoked a curt swear word from him as he lifted his mouth off her breast. 'I'd better get this. It's the ringtone I set up for Nonno's carer.' He pulled out his phone and took the call, a frown pulling at his forehead.

Artie rearranged her clothes and tried not to eavesdrop but it was impossible not to get the gist of the conversation. His grandfather had suffered a fall and was being taken to hospital with a suspected broken hip. Luca ended the call after reassuring his grandfather's carer he would leave for the hospital straight away.

He slipped the phone back in his pocket and gave Artie a grave look. 'You heard most of that?'

Artie placed her hand on his forearm. 'I'm so sorry. Is he going to be okay?'

He shrugged one shoulder, the almost casual action at odds with the dark shadows in his eyes. 'Who knows? Nonno is eighty-three. A broken hip is a big deal for someone of that age.' He released a breath and continued. 'I'm going to the hospital now. I want to speak to the orthopaedic surgeon. I want to make sure Nonno gets the very best of care.' He held her gaze for a moment. 'This might be your only chance to meet him.' His voice was husky with carefully contained emotion but she could sense the effort it took. His jaw was locked tight, his nostrils flaring as he fought to control his breathing.

Artie's throat tightened. 'I wish I could go with you, Luca. I really do.'

He gave a movement of his lips that wasn't quite a smile. He reached for her hand and gave it a gentle press. 'I'll be back as soon as I can.'

'Please send my best wishes for a speedy recovery.' Artie knew the words were little more than useless platitudes when all Luca wanted was her by his side. She was never more aware of letting down her side of the bargain. Letting *him* down. It pained her she was unable to harness her fear for his sake.

She watched as he drove away, her heart feeling as if it was torn in two. It felt wrong not to be with him—wrong in a way she hadn't expected to feel. As if part of her was missing now he was gone. The *castello* had never been more of a prison, her fear never more of a burden. Why couldn't she feel the fear and do it anyway? Was she to be imprisoned within these walls for the rest of her life? Luca needed her and she wasn't able to be with him, and yet she wanted nothing more than to be by his side.

She wanted to be with him because she loved him.

Artie could no longer suppress or deny her feelings about him. She had fallen in love with him in spite of his rules, in spite of her own efforts to keep her heart out of their arrangement. But her heart had been in it from the moment Luca kissed her. He had awoken her out of a psychological coma, inspiring her to live life in a full and vibrant way. How could she let him down now when he needed her? How could she not fight through her fears for him?

Rosa came out to join her, shading her eyes from the blinding sunshine. 'Do you know when he'll be back?'

Artie gave a despondent sigh. 'No. I feel so bad I wasn't able to go with him. What sort of wife am I that I can't even be by my husband's side when he needs me most?'

Rosa gave her a thoughtful look. 'I guess you have to measure up which thing is bigger—your fear of leaving here or your fear of not being there for him.'

Artie bit her lip, struggling to hold back a tumult of negative emotion. Her sense of failure, her lack of courage, her inability to overcome her phobia.

You're hopeless. A failure. An embarrassment.

Her harsh internal critic rained down abuse until she wanted to curl up into a tiny ball and hide away. But hiding never solved anything, did it? She had hidden here for ten years and nothing had changed.

And yet…something *had* changed. Luca had changed her. Awakening her to feelings and sensations she hadn't thought possible a few days ago. Feelings she could no longer hide from—feelings that were not part of Luca's rules but she felt them anyway. How could she not? He was the light to her darkness, the healing salve to her psychological wound, the promise of a life outside these cold stone walls. He was her gateway to the outside world, the world that had frightened and terrified her so much because she didn't trust it to keep her safe.

But she trusted Luca.

She had trusted him with her body, giving herself to him, responding to him with a powerful passion she could still feel in her most intimate flesh. Her love for him was bigger than her fear. Much bigger. That was what she would cling to as she stared down her demons. She had the will, she had the motivation, she had her love for him to empower her in a way nothing had been able to before. Luca was outside her prison walls, and the only way she could be with him in his hour of need was to leave the *castello*, propelled, empowered, galvanised by the love she felt for him.

Love was supposed to conquer all.

She would damn well prove it.

CHAPTER NINE

LUCA GOT TO the hospital in time to speak to his grandfather before he was taken for surgery. Nonno looked ashen and there was a large purple and black bruise on his face as well as his wrist and elbow where he had tried to break his fall. Luca took the old man's papery hand and tried to reassure him. 'I'll be here when you come out of theatre. Try not to worry.'

Nonno grimaced in pain and his eyes watered. 'When am I going to meet this new wife of yours? You'd better hurry up and bring her to me before I fall off my perch.'

'Soon,' Luca said, hoping it was true. 'When you're feeling better. You don't want to scare her off with all those bruises, do you?'

A wry smile played with the corners of Nonno's mouth. 'It's good that you've settled down, Luca. I've been worried about you since…well, for a long time now.'

'I know you have.' Luca patted his grandfather's hand, his chest tightening as if it were in a vice. 'I was waiting for the right one to come along. Just like you did with Nonna.'

The strange thing was, Artie did feel right. Right in so many ways. He couldn't imagine making love to anyone else, which was kind of weird, given there was a time limit on their relationship. A six-month time limit he insisted on because no way was he interested in being in for the long haul. Not with his track record of destroying people's lives.

'Your grandmother was a wonderful woman,' Nonno said, with a wistful look on his weathered features. 'I miss her every day.'

'I know you do, Nonno. I miss Nonna too.'

Another good reason not to love someone—the pain of losing them wrecked your life, leaving you alone and heartsore for years on end. If that wasn't a form of torture, what was? None Luca wanted any part of, not if he could help it.

He was already missing Artie, and he'd only been away from her the couple of hours it took to drive to the hospital. He'd wanted her to come with him to meet his grandfather but that wasn't the only reason. He genuinely enjoyed being with her, which was another new experience for him. The women he'd dated in the past were nice enough people, but no one had made him feel the way Artie did.

Making love with her had been like making love for the first time, discovering things about his body as well as hers. Being tuned in to his body in a totally different way, as if his response settings had been changed, ramped up, intensified, so he would want no one other than her. No one else could trigger the same need and drive. No one else would satisfy him the way she did. He ached for her now. What he would give to see her smile, to feel her hand slide into his and her body nestle against him.

His grandfather turned his head to lock gazes with Luca. 'I've been hard on you, Luca, over the years. I see it now when it's too late to do anything about it. I've expected a lot of you. You had to grow up too fast after your father and Angelo died.' He sighed and continued. 'You've worked hard, too hard really, but I know your father would be proud of your achievements. You've carried on his legacy and turned Ferrantelli Enterprises into a massive success.' He gave a tired smile.

'I've only ever wanted you to be happy. Success is good, but personal fulfilment is what life is really about.'

The hospital orderly arrived at that point to take Nonno down to the operating theatre.

Luca grasped his grandfather's hand and gave it a gentle squeeze. 'Try and get well again, Nonno. I'll be waiting here for you when you come back.'

Once his grandfather had been wheeled out of the room, Luca leaned back in the visitors' chair in his grandfather's private room and stretched out his legs and closed his eyes. Hospitals stirred emotions in him he didn't want to feel. It was a trigger response to tragedy. Being surrounded by death and disease and uncertainty caused an existential crisis in even the most level-headed of people. Being reminded of a loved one's mortality and your own. It would be a long wait until Nonno came out of theatre and then recovery but he wanted to be here when his grandfather came back. His gut churned and his heart squeezed and his breath caught.

If he came back…

Artie put her small overnight case in the back of Rosa's car and pressed the button to close the boot. She took a deep breath and mentally counted to three on releasing it. She came around to the passenger side and took another breath. 'Okay. I can do this.'

I have to do this. For Luca. For myself. For his grandfather.

She got in the car and pulled the seatbelt into place, her heart pounding, her skin prickling with beads of perspiration.

Rosa started the engine and shifted the gearstick into 'drive'. 'Are you sure about this?'

Artie nodded with grim determination. 'I'm sure. It won't be easy but I want to be with Luca. I need to be with him.'

Rosa drove towards the bronze gates, which opened automatically because of the sensors set on either side of the crushed limestone driveway. Artie concentrated on her breathing, trying to ignore the fear that was like thousands of sticky-footed ants crawling over her skin. Her chest was tight, her heart hammering like some sort of malfunctioning construction machinery, but she was okay… well, a little bit okay.

Rosa flicked a worried glance her way. 'How are you doing?'

Artie gripped the strap of the seatbelt that

crossed her chest. Her stomach had ditched the butterflies and recruited bats instead. Frantically flapping bats. 'So far, so good. Keep going. We're nearly outside.'

They drove the rest of the way out of the gates and Artie held her breath, anticipating a crippling flood of panic. But instead of the silent screams of terror inside her head, she heard Luca's calm, deep voice, coaching her through the waves of dread.

'Breathe, cara. *One. Two. Three.'*

It wasn't the first time someone had taught her breath control—two of the therapists had done so with minimal results. But for some reason Luca's voice was the one she listened to now. It gave her the courage to go further than she had gone in over a decade. Out through the *castello* gates and into the outside world.

Artie looked at Rosa and laughed. 'I did it! I'm out!'

Rosa blinked away tears. '*Sì*, you're out.'

Artie wished she could say the rest of the journey was easy. It was not. They had to stop so many times for her to get control of her panic. The nausea at one stage was so bad she thought she was going to vomit. She distracted herself with the sights and sounds along the way. Looking at views she never thought she would see again—the rolling, verdant fields, the lush forests and the mountains, the vineyards and orchards and olive groves of Umbria. Scenes from her childhood, places she had travelled past with her parents. The memories were happy and sad, poignant and painful, and yet also gave her a sense of closure. It was time to move on. Luca had given her the tools and the motivation to change her thinking, to shift her focus. And the further away from the *castello* they got, the easier it became, because she knew she was getting closer to Luca.

But then they came to the hospital.

Artie had forgotten about the hospital. Hospitals. Busyness. Crowds. People rushing about. Patients, staff, cleaners, security personnel. The dead, the dying and the injured. A vision of her mother's lifeless, bruised and broken body flashed into her brain. A vision of her father in the Critical Care Spinal Unit, his shattered spine no longer able to keep him upright.

Her fault. Her fault. Her fault.

She had destroyed her family.

Artie gripped the edges of her seat, her

heart threatening to pound its way out of her chest. 'I can't go in there. I can't.'

Rosa parked the car in the visitor's parking area and turned off the engine. 'You've come this far.'

'It was a mistake.' Artie closed her eyes so she didn't have to look at the front entrance. 'I can't do this. I'm not ready.'

I will never be ready.

'What if I call Luca to come out and get you?'

Artie opened her eyes and took a deep breath and slowly released it. Luca was inside that building. She was only a few metres away from him. She had come this far, further than she had in ten years. All she had to do was get to Luca. 'No. I'm not giving up now. I want to be with Luca more than anything. But I need to do this last bit on my own. You can go home and I'll talk to you in a few days once we know what's happening with Luca's grandfather.' She released her tight grip on the car seat and smoothed her damp palms down her thighs. 'I'm ready. I'm going in. Wish me luck?'

Rosa smiled and brushed some tears away from her eyes with the back of her hand. 'You've got this.'

* * *

Luca opened his eyes when he heard the door of his grandfather's room open, but instead of seeing a nurse come in he saw Artie. For a moment he thought he was dreaming. He blinked and blinked again then sprang out of the chair, taking her by the arms to make sure she was actually real and not a figment of his imagination. '*Cara?* How did you get here? I can barely believe my eyes.'

She smiled, her eyes bright, her cheeks flushed pink. 'Rosa brought me. I wanted to be with you. I forced myself to get here. I can't say it was easy. It was awful, actually. But I kept doing the slow breathing thing and somehow I made it.'

Luca gathered her close to his chest, breathing in the flowery scent of her hair where it tickled his chin. He was overcome with emotion, thinking about the effort it must have cost her to stare down her fears.

For him?

Fears she had lived with for ten years and she had pushed through them to get to his side. To be with him while he faced the very real possibility of losing his grandfather. He wasn't sure how it made him feel…awed, honoured, touched in a way he had rarely been touched. He was used to having entirely transactional relationships with people. He took what he wanted and they did too.

But Artie had given him something no one had ever done before—her complete trust.

'You were very brave, *mia piccola*. It's so good to have you here.' He held her apart from him to smile down at her, a locked space inside his chest flaring open. 'I still can't believe it.' He brushed his bent knuckles down her cheek. 'Nonno will be so pleased to meet you.'

Her forehead creased in concern. 'How is he? Did you get to speak to him before—?'

'Yes, he's in Theatre, or maybe in Recovery by now.' Luca took both of her hands in his. 'I've missed you.'

'I've missed you too.' Her voice whisper-soft, her gaze luminous.

He released her hands and gathered her close again, lowering his mouth to hers in a kiss that sent scorching streaks of heat shooting through his body. She pressed herself closer, her mouth opening to the probe of his tongue. Tingles went down the backs of his legs, blood thundered to his groin, rampant need pounding in his system. Her lips tasted of strawberries and milk with a touch of cinnamon, her little gasps of delight sweet music to his ears and fuel for his desire. A desire that burned and boiled and blistered with incendiary heat right throughout his body in pummelling waves. How could one kiss do so much damage? Light such a fire in his flesh?

Because it was *her* kiss.

Her mouth.

Her.

Luca lifted his mouth off hers to look down at her flushed features and shimmering eyes. 'If we weren't in my grandfather's hospital room, I would show you just how much I've missed you right here and now.'

Her cheeks went a delightful shade of pink. 'I've sent Rosa back home. It's okay for me to stay with you, isn't it?'

Luca smiled. 'I can think of nothing I'd like more. My villa is only half an hour from here.'

She stroked his face with her fingers, sending darts of pleasure through his body. 'Thank you for helping me move past my fear. I know it's still early days, and I know I'll probably have lots of setbacks, but I feel like I'm finally moving in the right direction.'

Luca tucked a loose strand of her hair back behind her ear, feeling like someone had spilled warm honey into his chest cavity. 'I'm so proud of you right now. The first steps are always the hardest in any difficult journey.'

Artie toyed with the open collar of his shirt, her eyes not quite meeting his. 'I found it helped to shift my focus off myself and put it on you instead. I knew you wanted me with you and I wanted to be with you too. So, so much. That had to be a bigger driver than my fear of leaving the *castello*. And thankfully, it was.'

Luca framed her face in his hands, meshing his gaze with hers. 'Once Nonno is out of danger, I am going to introduce you to everything you've only dreamed of until now.'

She wound her arms around his neck and stepped up on tiptoe to plant a soft kiss to his mouth. 'I can hardly wait.'

A short time later, Luca's grandfather was wheeled back into the room. Artie held on to Luca's hand, feeling nervous at meeting the old man for the first time. She had met so few people over the last decade and had lost the art of making small talk. But she drew strength from having Luca by her side and basked in his pride in her for making it to the hospital. Something had shifted in their relationship, a subtle shift that gave her more confidence around him. He might not love her but he wanted her with him and that was more than enough for now.

It *had* to be enough.

Her love for him might seem sudden, but wasn't that how it happened for some people? An instant attraction, a chemistry that couldn't be denied, an unstoppable force. Luca didn't believe himself capable of loving someone, but then, she hadn't believed herself capable of being able to leave the *castello*. But she had left. She had found the courage within to do so. Would it not be the same for him? He would need to find the courage to love without fear.

Nonno groaned and cranked one eye open. 'Luca?'

Luca moved forward, taking Artie with him. He took his grandfather's hand in his. 'I'm here, Nonno. And so is Artie.'

The old man turned his head on the pillow and his sleepy gaze brightened. 'Ah, my dear girl. I'm so glad to meet you in person. I hope you'll be as happy with Luca as I was with my Marietta.'

Artie stepped closer. '*Buongiorno*, Signor

Ferrantelli. It is so lovely to meet you face to face.'

The old man grasped her hand. 'Call me Nonno. You're family now, *sì*?'

Family. If only Nonno knew how short a time she would be a part of the Ferrantelli family. Artie smiled and squeezed his hand back in a gesture of warm affection. 'Yes, Nonno. I'm family now.'

An hour or so later, Luca drove Artie to his sprawling estate in Tuscany a few kilometres from the town of San Gimignano, where fourteen of the once seventy-two medieval towers created an ancient skyline. The countryside outside the medieval town was filled with sloping hills and lush valleys interspersed with slopes of grapevines and olive groves and fields of bright red poppies. Tall pines stood like sentries overlooking the verdant fields and the lowering sun cast a golden glow over the landscape, the angle of light catching the edges of the cumulous clouds and sending shafts and bolts of gold down to the earth in a spectacular fashion.

Artie drank in the view, feeling over-awed by the beauty to the point of tears. She brushed at her eyes and swallowed a lump in her throat. 'It's so beautiful…the colours, the light—everything. I can't believe I'm seeing it in real time instead of through a screen or the pages of a book or magazine.' She turned to him. 'Do you mind if we stop for a minute? I want to stand by the roadside and smell the air and listen to the sounds of nature.'

'Sure.' Luca stopped the car and came around to open her door. He took her hand and helped her out of the car, a smile playing at the corners of his mouth, creating attractive crinkles near his eyes. 'It's an amazing part of the country, isn't it?'

'It sure is.' Artie stood beside him on the roadside and lifted her face to feel the dance of the evening breeze. She breathed in the scent of wild grasses and sun-warmed pine trees. Listened to the twittering of birds, watched an osprey ride the warm currents of air as it searched for prey below. A swell of emotion filled Artie's chest that Luca had helped her leave the prison of her past. 'I never thought I'd be able to do things like this again.'

Luca put an arm around her waist and gathered her closer against his side. 'I'm proud of you. It can't have been easy, but look at you now.'

She glanced up at him and smiled. 'I don't know how to thank you.'

'I can think of a way.' His eyes darkened and his mouth came down to press a lingering kiss to hers. After a few breathless moments, he lifted his mouth from hers and smiled. 'We'd better get going before it gets dark.'

Once they were back in the car and on their way again, he placed her hand on the top of his thigh and her fingers tingled at the hard warmth of his toned muscles beneath her palm. 'Thank you for being so sweet to Nonno,' he went on. 'He already loves you. You remind him of my grandmother.'

Artie basked in the glow of his compliment. 'What was she like? Were you close to her?'

His expression was like the sky outside—shifting shadows as the light gradually faded. 'I was close to her in the early days, before my father and brother drowned. Their deaths hit her hard and she lost her spark and never quite got it back.' His hands tightened on the steering wheel, making his knuckles bulge to white knobs of tension. 'Like my mother, being around me reminded her too much of what she'd lost. I was always relieved when it was time to go back to boarding school and even more so when I moved away for university.'

Artie stroked his thigh in a comforting fashion, her heart contracting for the way he had suffered as a young teenager. She was all too familiar with how grief and guilt were a deadly combination. Destroying hope, suffocating any sense of happiness or fulfilment. 'I can only imagine how hard it was for all of you, navigating your way through so much grief. But what about your mother? You said she lives in New York now. Do you ever see her?'

'Occasionally, when I'm there for work.' His mouth twisted. 'It's…difficult being with her, as it is for her to be with me.'

'I don't find it hard to be with you.' The words were out of her mouth before she could stop them. She bit her lip and mentally cringed as heat flooded her cheeks. Next she would be blurting out how much she loved him. Words he clearly didn't want to hear. Love wasn't part of their six-month arrangement. Romantic love wasn't part of his life, period.

Luca glanced her way, a smile tilting the edges of his mouth and his eyes dark and warm. 'I don't find it hard to be with you either.' His voice was low and deep and husky and made her long to be back in his arms. To feel the sensual power of his body, the physical expression of his need, even if love wasn't part of why he desired her. But she realised now her desire was a physical manifestation of her love for him. A love that had awakened the first time his lips touched hers, waking her from a psychological coma. A coma where she had denied herself the right to fully engage in life and relationships. Locking herself away out of fear. But she was free now, freed by Luca's passion for her and hers for him.

'Will I get to meet your mother? I mean, is that something you'd like me to do?' Artie asked.

A frown formed a double crease between his eyes. 'I'm not sure it will achieve much.'

'But what if I'd like to?'

He flicked her a brief unreadable glance. 'Why do you want to?'

Artie sighed. 'I lost my mother when I was fifteen. It left such a hole in my life. I can barely watch a television show or commercials or movies with mothers in them because it makes me miss my mother all the more.'

'You have no need to be envious of my relationship with my mother,' Luca said in a weighted tone.

'At least you still have her.'

There was a protracted silence.

Luca released a heavy breath. 'Look, I know you are only trying to help but some family dynamics are best left alone. Nothing can be changed now.'

'But that's what I thought about my fear of leaving the *castello*,' Artie said. 'I lost years of my life by giving in to my fears, allowing them to control me instead of me controlling them. I never thought I could do it, but you helped me see that I could. Maybe it's the same with your relationship with your mother. You shouldn't give up on trying to improve the relationship just because it's been a little difficult so far. What you went through as a family was horrendously tragic. But you still have a family, Luca. You have your mother and your grandfather. I have no one now.'

Luca reached for her hand and brought it up to his mouth, pressing a soft kiss to her fingers. 'You have me, *cara*.' His voice had a note of tenderness that made her heart contract.

But for how long? Six months and no longer. And then she would be alone again.

* * *

A short time later, Luca drove through the gates of his estate and pulled up in front of the imposing medieval villa.

Built like a fortress with four storeys, a central dome and several turrets, it was surrounded by landscaped gardens with a tinkling fountain at the front. 'Don't be put off by the grim façade,' he said, turning off the engine. 'I've done extensive renovations inside.'

'I try never to judge a book or a person by their cover,' Artie said. 'Not that I've met a lot of people lately, but still. Hopefully that's going to change.'

Luca's eyes glinted. 'I'm not sure I want to share you with anyone just yet. This is our honeymoon, *si*?'

A shiver coursed down Artie's spine and a pool of liquid fire simmered in her core. She sent him a shy smile. 'So, we'll be alone here? Just you and me?'

He leaned closer across the gear shaft and, putting a hand to the back of her head, brought her closer to his descending mouth. 'Just you and me.'

CHAPTER TEN

ARTIE WOKE THE next morning to find her head tucked against Luca's chest and his arms around her and her legs tangled with his. One of his hands was moving up and down her spine in a slow stroking motion that made her pelvis start to tingle. His hand went lower, to the curve of her bottom, and every nerve in her skin did a happy dance. Her inner muscles woke to his touch, instantly recalling the magic of the night before and wanting more. Would she ever tire of feeling his hands on her body? His touch was gentle and yet created a storm in her flesh. A tumult of sensations that made her ache for closer, deeper, more intimate contact.

Luca turned her onto her back and leaned on one elbow to gaze down at her. He brushed some wayward strands of her hair back from her face, his eyes darkly hooded, a lazy smile tipping up one side of his mouth. 'Well, look who's been sleeping in my bed.' His voice had a sexy early-morning rasp to it that made something in her belly turn over.

Artie traced a straight line down his strong nose, a playful smile tilting her own mouth. 'I don't know that I did much sleeping.' Her finger began to circle his stubble-surrounded mouth and chin. 'Unless I was dreaming about you making love to me...how many times was it?'

His eyes darkened. 'Three.' He stroked her bottom lip with his thumb, a small frown settling between his brows. 'I would have gone for four or even five but I didn't want to make you sore. This is all so new to you and...'

Artie smoothed his frown away with her finger. 'New, but wonderful.' She looked deep into his eyes, holding her hand against his prickly jaw. 'I didn't think it would be so... so wonderful. Is it always like this?'

Luca held her gaze for a long moment, his eyes moving between each of hers before lowering to her mouth. He released a soft gust of air, his lopsided smile returning. 'No. It's not always as good as this.'

'Really? Are you just saying that to make me feel good?'

He picked up one of her hands and turned it over to plant a kiss to the middle of her palm, his eyes holding hers. 'I'm saying it because it's true. It feels…different with you.'

'In what way?'

He interlaced his fingers with hers, a contemplative frown interrupting his features. 'I can't explain it. It just feels different.'

Artie aimed her gaze at his mouth rather than meet his eyes. 'Is it because of my lack of experience? I must seem a bit of a novelty to someone like you who's had so many lovers.'

He tipped up her chin and his eyes met hers, and something shifted in the atmosphere. A new, electric energy, a background hum, as if each and every oxygen particle had paused to take a breath.

'I'm not going to dismiss any of my past lovers to faceless bodies who didn't leave a single impression on me, because it's simply not true.'

He stroked his thumb over her lower lip again—a slow-motion stroke that set her mouth buzzing.

'But with you…it feels like I'm discovering sex for the first time. Feeling things on a different level. A more intense level.'

Artie toyed with the hair at the back of his neck, her lower body tinglingly aware of the growing ridge of his erection. Aware of the potent energy that pulsed and throbbed between them. 'I couldn't have asked for a better first lover.'

His mouth came down and sealed hers in a mind-altering kiss that set her pulse racing. His fingers splayed through her hair, his tongue meeting hers in a playful dance with distinctive erotic overtones. Her lower body quaked with longing, her flesh recognising the primal call to connect in the most physically intimate way of all. Her legs tangled with his rougher ones, her breasts crushed against the firm wall of his chest, her nipples already tightening into pert buds.

One of Luca's hands cradled one of her breasts, his touch light, and yet it sent shockwaves of need coursing through her body. Molten heat was licking along her flesh… lightning-fast zaps and tingles that made her groan in pleasure. She moved closer, pressing her mound to his erection, opening her legs for him, desperate to have him inside her.

'Not so impatient, *cara*.' He gave a light laugh and reached for protection, deftly applying it before coming back to her, his eyes gleaming with the fiery desire she could feel roaring through her own body.

Artie framed his head in her hands, her breathing erratic. 'I want you so much it's like pain.'

'I want you too. Badly.' He kissed her mouth in a kiss that spoke of his own thrumming desire, his lips firm, insistent, hungry.

He moved down her body, kissing her breasts, her belly, and to the secret heart of her womanhood. He separated her and anointed her with his lips and tongue, making her writhe and gasp with bone-melting pleasure. The wave broke over her in a rush, sending her spinning into a place of sheer physical bliss. The storm in her flesh slowly abated but then he created another one by moving up her body again, entering her with a slow, deep thrust that made every hair on her head tingle and tighten at the roots. Her back arched, her thighs trembled, her breath stalled and then came out in a rush of rapturous delight. Delicious sensations rippled through her as he continued to thrust, his breathing rate increasing along with his pace, his touch like fire where his hand was holding her hip, tilting her to him. The pressure built in her body, the primal need a drumbeat working its way up to a powerful crescendo. Blood pounded through her veins, a hot rush fuelled by the intense sensations activated by the erotic friction of his hard male body.

Artie lifted her hips to get him where she most wanted him but it was still not quite the pressure she needed. 'I'm so close…so damn close…'

'Relax, *mia piccola*. Don't fight it.' Luca slipped a hand between their bodies and stroked the swollen heart of her flesh, sending her over the edge into a cataclysmic orgasm that surpassed everything she had enjoyed so far. Starlight burst behind her eyelids, fireworks exploded in her body, heat pouring like liquid flames all through her pelvis and down her legs to curl her toes.

'Oh, God. Oh, God. Oh, God,' she panted, like she had run a marathon, her heart pounding, her flesh tinglingly alive with mind-smashing ecstasy.

Luca's release followed hers and swept her up in its power and intensity. His entire body seemed to tighten as if he were poised on the edge of a vertiginous cliff. And then he gave an agonised groan and shuddered as if consumed with a rabid fever, his essence spilling, his body finally relaxing against hers.

Artie stroked her hands down his back where his firm flesh was still peppered with goosebumps. The in and out of his breath tickled the side of her neck but she didn't want to move in case it broke the magical spell washing over her, binding her to him in a way no words could possibly describe. There was a rightness about their union—a sense of belonging together for all time.

But you've only got six months, remember?

The prod of her conscience froze her breath and stopped her heart for a moment. It wasn't long enough. Six months was a joke. She wanted for ever. She wanted to be in his arms like this for the rest of her life. How could she ever move on from her relationship with him? Who would ever measure up? How could she love anyone else when he had stolen her heart from the first time he kissed her?

She didn't want to love anyone else. Her heart belonged to him and only him.

Luca must have sensed the subtle change in her mood, and quickly disposed of the condom, and then leaned up on one elbow to look at her, his hand idly brushing her wild hair out of her face. 'What's wrong?' His tone and gaze were gently probing.

Artie painted a smile on her lips. 'Nothing.'

His eyes moved between each of hers like a powerful searchlight looking for something hidden in the shadows. His thumb began to stroke the pillow of her lower lip in slow movements that sent hot tingles through every corridor of her flesh. 'I've been around long enough to know that "nothing" usually means "something". Talk to me, *cara*. Tell me what's worrying you.'

She aimed her gaze at his Adam's apple, her heart skipping rope in her chest. How could she be honest with him without relaying how she felt? He might call an end to their physical relationship and go back to the paper marriage he'd first insisted on. 'I'm just wondering how I will ever find another lover who makes me feel the way you do. I mean, in the future, when we're done.'

There was a beat or two of thick silence.

Then Luca's hand fell away from her face and he released a heavy sigh and rolled onto his back, one arm flung over the edge of the bed, the other coming up to cover his eyes. 'The last thing I want to think about right now is you with someone else.' There was a rough quality to his voice that hinted at a fine thread of anger running under the surface.

'But it's going to happen one day,' Artie

said. 'We're both going to move on with our lives. Isn't that what you planned? What you insisted on?'

He removed his arm from across his face and sat upright, the muscles of his abdomen rippling like coils of steel. He swung his legs over the edge of the bed, his hands resting on either side of his thighs, his back towards her, his head and shoulders hunched forward as if he was fighting to control his emotions.

There was another tight silence.

Artie swallowed, wondering if she had pushed him too far. 'Luca?' She reached out and stroked her hand down between his tense shoulder blades, and he flinched as if her touch burned him. 'What's wrong?'

'Nothing.' The word was bitten out. Hard. Blunt. *Keep-away* curt.

She had a strange desire to smile—her lips twitched as she tried to control it. What was sauce for the goose and all that. 'You know, someone told me recently that "nothing" usually means "something".'

Luca let out a gush of air and gave a deep, self-deprecating chuckle. He turned back to face her. 'Touché.' He took her nearest hand and brought it up to his mouth, locking his gaze with hers. He bit down gently on the end of her index finger and then drew it into his mouth, sucking on it erotically. She shivered and a wave of heat passed through her body, simmering, smouldering like hot coals in her core.

He released her finger from his mouth and returned to holding her hand in his. 'Sometimes I wonder if I need my head read for allowing this to go this far between us.' His thumb stroked over the fleshy part of her thumb, the back-and-forth motion making her stomach do a flip turn. 'But I can't seem to stop myself from wanting you.'

Artie leaned closer, placing her free hand on the rock-hard wall of his chest, her mouth just below his. 'Want me all you like.' She pressed her lips to his in a barely-there kiss, pulling back to gaze into his eyes. 'We've got six months.'

She kept her tone light. *I'm-totally-cool-with-having-a-time-limit-on-our-relationship* light.

He held her gaze for a long moment, shadows shifting in his eyes like filtered sunlight moving across a forest floor. Then his eyes lowered to her mouth, a muscle in his cheek pulsing as if something wasn't quite at peace within him. 'Then let's make the most of it,' he said and covered her mouth with his.

The following evening, after spending some time visiting Nonno, Luca took Artie out for dinner at a restaurant in San Gimignano with a spectacular view over the region. She sat opposite him at a table at the window at the front of the restaurant, feeling both nervous and excited about her first meal out at a restaurant since she was a teenager.

Artie took a sip of the crisp white wine Luca had ordered, and then surveyed the menu. 'So much to choose from…'

'Take your time.' His tone was indulgent, as if he sensed how overawed she was feeling.

Once their orders were taken by the waiter, Artie glanced up at Luca with a rueful expression. 'I'm frightened I might use the wrong cutlery or something. It's been so long since I've eaten in public. I'm glad the restaurant isn't busy tonight.'

He reached for her hand across the table, holding it gently in the cradle of his. 'I made sure it wasn't busy. I know the owner. I asked him to keep this part of the restaurant clear for us.'

Artie blinked at him in surprise. 'Really?

But wouldn't that have incurred a considerable loss of income for him?'

Luca shrugged one broad shoulder. 'Don't worry. I've more than compensated him.'

She chewed at the side of her mouth, touched that Luca had gone to so much trouble and expense for her comfort. 'I guess I can hardly call myself a cheap date, now, can I?'

His fingers squeezed hers, a smile playing about his mouth. 'You're worth more than you realise, *cara*. My grandfather certainly thinks so—he was in much better spirits today. Meeting you has done him the power of good. He told me when you were using the bathroom earlier today that he's decided to go ahead with the chemo for his cancer. I have you to thank for his change in attitude. He wants to live now. You've given him a reason to.'

'I'm so glad,' Artie said. 'But I hope the chemo won't be too gruelling. He's not a young man.'

'No, but he's a tough old guy.' Luca stroked his thumb over the back of her hand and added in a heavy tone, 'It's something I've been dreading—losing him. He's the last link to my father and brother, apart from my mother, of course.'

Artie could sense the deep love he had for his grandfather and it gave her hope that he might one day learn to embrace other forms of love—romantic love. Love-for-a-lifetime love. *Her* love.

'Has your mother been to see Nonno recently?'

His mouth twisted, a shadow passing through his gaze. 'They talk on the phone now and again. My mother hates flying back to Italy. It reminds her too much of our flight back from Argentina with my father's and brother's bodies.' He released her hand and picked up his wine glass, staring at the golden liquid with a frowning expression.

Artie placed her hand on his other forearm where it was resting on the table. 'I can only imagine how devastated you both were on that trip home. I can relate to it with my own journey home from hospital after the accident. It felt surreal, like I was having a nightmare or something. I kept expecting my mother to be there when I got home, but of course she wasn't. And my father was a shell of himself. A broken shell. I blamed myself, just as you did and still do.'

Luca leaned forward and took both of her hands in his. 'We've both suffered terrible tragedies. Nothing is going to change the past. It's done and can't be undone. But it's important to live your own life.'

Artie looked down at their joined hands. 'At least I'm living my life now, thanks to you. I think I was asleep to myself for the last ten years.' She raised her gaze to his and continued, 'I didn't realise how much I'd let my fear control me. It kind of crept up on me until I was completely imprisoned by it. But somehow you got me to change my focus, to shift my thinking. How can I ever thank you for that?'

'You don't have to thank me. You did it all by yourself.' Luca idly stroked her hands with his thumbs. 'You're doing so well now. I can't tell you how shocked and delighted I was to see you appear at the hospital the other day. I thought I was dreaming.'

'I was sick with nerves,' Artie confessed. 'But knowing you were there at the end of my journey really helped. It gave me a clear goal to aim for.'

Luca smiled and released one of her hands, then took a flat rectangular jewellery box out of his jacket pocket. 'I have something for you.' He placed the box on the table between them. 'Open it.'

Artie prised open the lid to find a beautiful diamond and sapphire pendant and matching earrings. 'Oh, Luca, they're absolutely gorgeous!' She picked up one of the dangling earrings. 'But they're the same design as your grandmother's engagement ring. Does that mean they're—?'

'*Sì*, they were Nonna's. I want you to have the whole collection.'

'But they're priceless heirlooms. Why are you giving them to me?'

'Don't you think you're worth it?'

She put the earring back in the box, and ran her fingertip over the fine gold chain of the pendant. 'It's not that so much…' She glanced up at him. 'It's more that I feel uncomfortable with you being so generous to me when we're only going to be together for six months. I mean, I seem to be the biggest winner in this arrangement of ours. I get to keep the *castello* and all this amazing jewellery, and what do you get?'

His eyes held hers in a strange little lock that made the hairs on the back of her neck tingle. 'I get some wonderful memories of our time together. Plus, my grandfather will hopefully recover now he's agreed to go ahead with the treatment.'

Artie frowned. 'But don't you want more than that?'

A screen came up in his gaze. 'What more could I want?'

Me. You could want me, for ever.

Artie couldn't bring herself to say it out loud but she wondered if he could hear her hopes in the ringing silence. 'Don't you want to keep your grandmother's jewellery in case one day you change your mind about marrying someone else?'

'Not going to happen.' He sat back in his chair, lifted his wine glass from the table and took a measured sip. 'I have no plans of that nature.'

Not going to happen.

The words taunted her for the rest of the meal.

Not going to happen.

He was so adamant about never falling in love.

Not going to happen.

How could he be so confident it wouldn't happen?

And how could she be so hopeful it would? That he would fall in love with her?

CHAPTER ELEVEN

ONCE DINNER WAS OVER, Luca led the way back to his car past a wine bar where live music was being played. The sweet strains of a well-known Italian love song filled the night air. He glanced down at Artie's wistful expression, and stopped in front of the entrance. 'Do you fancy going in for a bit?'

She shifted from foot to foot, looking like she was torn between running away and going in and letting her hair down. 'I haven't heard live music before. And I've never been to a wine bar. Or danced with anyone before.'

He took her hand and looped it through his arm. 'Come on, then. Let's dance.'

A short time later, Luca held Artie in his arms as they slow-waltzed to another old love song. Her head was resting against his chest, her hair tickling his chin, her flowery fragrance teasing his nostrils. Her body moved in perfect time with his, as if they had been dancing together for ever. The naturalness of their motion reminded him of the natural rhythm of their lovemaking. It was as if their bodies were in tune with each other, recognising the other as the perfect partner.

Perfect partner? You're hardly that.

The sharp prod of his conscience made him miss a step and he had to gather Artie closer to stop her from bumping into another couple on the small dance floor. 'Sorry,' he said. 'I lost my concentration.' Or maybe he'd momentarily lost his mind, thinking about the possibility of a future with her.

A future he couldn't offer her.

When he'd first offered her a six-month marriage it had seemed an inordinately long time to be tied to someone, and yet now it didn't seem long enough. He avoided thinking about their inevitable divorce. Avoided thinking about a time when she wouldn't be in his life. Avoided thinking about her with someone else. He felt sick to his guts at the thought of her making love with some other man. He'd never considered himself the jealous type but he couldn't stomach the thought of her with someone else. What if they didn't treat her with respect? What if they weren't patient with her struggles in public? What if they didn't understand how sensitive and caring she was?

Artie looked up at him with luminous eyes, her face wreathed in smiles. 'This is so much fun. Can we do this another night soon?'

Luca smiled and bent his head to kiss her. 'I can think of nothing I'd like more.'

The next couple of weeks passed in a whirlwind of activity where Artie's feet barely touched the ground. There were visits to the hospital to see Luca's grandfather, who was making good progress after his hip surgery. Then there were trips to various sightseeing spots, and picnics in the countryside overlooking the hills and valleys of the region. Luca taught her about the skill of wine-making and olive production and showed her the vines and groves on his estate. He took her for romantic dinners in award-winning restaurants as well as less famous ones, where the food was just as fabulous and the atmosphere intimate and cosy. Luca took her shopping and spoilt her with a completely new wardrobe of clothes, including a collection of swimsuits and gorgeous lingerie.

But it was the nights at home she enjoyed

the most. Just being with him, sitting in the salon chatting, watching a movie or listening to music together, her head resting on his chest and his arms around her. It gave her a glimpse of what life could be like if they stayed together longer than the six months he'd stipulated. He was still driven by work and was often on the phone or answering emails, but she noticed he was more relaxed than before and seemed to smile and laugh more. Was it because his grandfather was on the mend and had decided to go ahead with his cancer treatment? Or was it because she had helped Luca to see there was more to life than work? That being in a romantic relationship could be positive rather than negative?

Artie had to bite her tongue so many times to stop herself from confessing how she felt about him but she let her actions do the talking instead. Every time she kissed him, she let her lips communicate her love. Every touch of her hands, every stroke of her fingers, every press of her body on his, love poured out of her. But she wanted to say it out loud. She needed to say it out loud. She needed him to hear the words—I love you.

They were sitting on the sofa watching the moon rise through the salon windows after a day of sightseeing. The moonlight cast a silver light over the surface of the infinity pool outside on the terrace overlooking the vineyard. Luca's arm was around her shoulders, her head resting on his shoulder, and soft music was playing through the sound system—cellos, violins and the sweetly lilting tones of a flute. A romantic ballad that tugged at her heartstrings and made her wish there wasn't a limit on their time together.

'Luca?'

'Mmm?' One of his hands began to play with her hair, sending shivers coursing down her spine.

Artie tilted her head to look at him. 'Luca, I want to talk to you about something. Something important.'

He brushed an imaginary hair away from her face, his eyes dark and serious. 'Go on.' His tone held a note of caution, unease, guardedness, but she refused to let it daunt her.

She swallowed a tight knot in her throat. 'There's so much I enjoy about being with you. You've spoilt me like a princess. You've treated me with so much patience and kindness and helped me build my confidence.'

He gave a half-smile, some of the wariness in his gaze fading. 'I like seeing you blossom, *cara*. You're a beautiful person who's been hiding away for too long.'

Artie touched his face with her fingers, her love for him taking up all the room in her chest so she could barely take a breath. 'I never thought I'd meet someone like you. And not just because I was locked away in the *castello*. But because I didn't think people as wonderful as you existed.'

Luca took her by the upper arms in a firm grip, his expression clouding. 'Look, don't go making me out to be a hero, Artie. I'm hardly that. You're confusing good chemistry with…other feelings.' Even the way he hesitated over the rest of his sentence showed how reluctant he was to the notion of love, but Artie pressed on regardless.

'Luca…' She took a deep breath and plunged in. 'I don't want our relationship to be temporary. I want more, and deep down I think you do too.'

His hands fell away from her arms and he sprang off the sofa to put some distance between them. 'You're wrong, Artie. That's not what I want. I've never wanted that. We made an agreement—'

Artie jumped off the sofa as well and stood in front of him. 'We made an agreement and then we changed it to what it is now—a physical relationship that works on every level but the one that means the most to me. I can't make love with you and keep my feelings to one side. They *are* the reason I want to make love with you. The only reason. I love you.'

Luca drew in a harsh-sounding breath and released it in a stuttered stream. He placed his hands on his hips, his shoulders hunched forward. 'You're young and inexperienced, of course, you're going to think the first person who makes love to you is the love of your life. But believe me, I am not that person.' His expression was like a walled fortress. Closed. Locked.

Keep out or face the consequences.

'You are that person.' Artie choked over the words as emotion welled in her throat. 'You've been that person from the moment we kissed at our wedding. Something happened that day—I knew it on a cellular level. And—'

'Will you listen to yourself?' His tone had a cutting edge that sliced at her self-esteem like a switchblade. 'You're spouting forth a fairy-tale fantasy. It's not real, Artie. You've fashioned me into some sort of romantic hero who ticks all the boxes for you. You need more life experience. You need to date other men so you can gain more perspective. You'll thank me in the end. Tying yourself to me indefinitely would be a mistake. A mistake you'll regret for the rest of your life.' He turned away from her, drawing in another ragged breath, his tone softening. 'Let's leave this for now. I don't want to upset you.'

Artie swallowed a tight restriction in her throat, tears stinging at the backs of her eyes. 'But you've already upset me by not accepting that I love you. You've dismissed it as if I don't know my own mind. I know what I feel.' She banged her fist against her chest for emphasis. 'I can't deny my feelings or ignore them as you seem to do. They're here with me all the time.'

Luca turned back around and opened and closed his eyes in a slow, *God-give-me-strength* blink. 'Look, you're one of the nicest people I've ever met, *cara*. You have so much to offer and I want you to be happy. I really do. But I'm not the person to make you happy. It's not in my skill set. I don't want the same things as you.'

Artie pressed her lips together for a moment to stop them from trembling. 'I think you do want the same things but you don't feel you deserve them because of what happened to your father and brother. I understand that more than most people, because I've experienced the same guilt for the last ten years. It completely imprisoned me, kept me from having a life of my own. But meeting you changed that. You freed me from my prison of fear and showed me I could have more than I ever thought possible.' She came up to him and placed her hand on his forearm. 'I know you have deep feelings locked away inside you. I feel it every time you kiss me. I feel it every time you make love to me.'

Luca brushed off her arm as if it was soiling his sleeve, his gaze hard, his mouth tight, his firewall still up. 'You're mistaking good sex for something else. It's an easy mistake to make, especially when you're not very experienced. But in time, you'll gain experience and realise this is just a crush, an infatuation that can't last.'

'I don't have to be experienced to know how I feel,' Artie said. 'They're *my* feelings. I feel them. I own them.'

'And I know how I feel and it doesn't include the sort of love you're talking about.' He ran a hand over his face and continued, 'I care about you, of course. I enjoy being with you but that's all it is—companionship and mutual desire that has an end point, as per our agreement.'

Artie's heart gave a painful spasm, and for a moment she couldn't locate her voice. He cared about her and enjoyed being with her but that was all it was? How could she have got it so wrong? She was sure he was developing feelings for her—sure enough to reveal her own. He thought her young and gauche, a girl in the throes of her first crush. How could she get through to him? How could she prove she loved him? Or was it pointless? Was she fooling herself that he would one day change? Didn't so many deluded women fall for that fantasy? The vain hope that in time, enough love would change their difficult men to the man of their dreams?

But what if Luca never changed?

What if he was incapable of it?

'Luca, I took a huge risk in leaving the *castello* for you,' Artie said. 'Why can't you take a risk and allow yourself to feel what I know is in your heart? I know it's scary to admit how much you care about someone. And I know the last thing you want to do is be reckless and spontaneous but we've connected in a way people rarely do. Surely you can't deny it? We have so much in common, can't you see that? We're perfect for each other.'

Luca turned his back, drawing in a deep breath, his hands on his hips in a braced position. 'Stop it, Artie. This is a pointless discussion. You're making me out to be someone I can never be.'

Artie ran her tongue over her dry lips, tasting the metallic bitterness of disappointment. She clasped her hands together in front of her body, trying to contain the emotions rioting through her. 'You'll never be free of the prison of the past unless you learn to let go of control. To allow yourself to be reckless with your heart, to open it to the feelings I know you've buried there. I've let go of control. I've opened my heart to you. Why can't you do it for me? If you won't do it for me, then it wouldn't be fair to either of us to continue in a relationship that is so out of balance.'

'It's not out of balance.' Luca swung back around to face her. 'I made it so we both get what we want. At the end of six months, you get to keep the *castello* and Nonno completes his chemo. It's a win-win.'

She shook her head at him. 'It's a lose-lose but you can't see it. I would choose love over a run-down old castle any day. And how are you going to explain the end of our marriage to your grandfather?'

He gave a dismissive shrug. 'Marriages break up all the time. It won't matter by then because he'll have finished the course of treatment. As I said—win-win.' His tone had a businesslike ring to it. No emotions. Ticking a box. Deal done.

Artie steepled her fingers around her nose and mouth, concentrating on keeping calm even though inside she was crumbling, the very foundations of her under assault as self-doubts rained down on her. She wasn't worthy of his love. She wasn't good enough. She was defective, damaged. He didn't love her. He would *never* love her. He had only married her as a means to an end, and yet she had fooled herself he was developing feelings for her. She was a fool for thinking he felt more for her than companionship and care.

Her old friend panic crept up behind her... lurking in the background.

You can't survive on your own. Stay with him. Put up and shut up.

Her skin prickled, fear slid into her stomach and coiled around her intestines, squeezing, tightening.

You'll lose the castello if you leave him now.

But Artie knew she couldn't lock herself in another prison. Staying with Luca in a loveless marriage for the next few months would be the same as locking herself in the *castello*. Shutting herself away from her hopes and dreams. From her potential.

From love.

She couldn't go back to being that frightened person now. She had to forge her way through with the strength and courage Luca had inspired in her. He had awakened her to what she most wanted in life and it would be wrong to go backwards, to silence the hopes and dreams she harboured. She owed it to herself to embrace life. To live life fully instead of living in negative solitude.

Artie lowered her hands from her face and straightened her shoulders, meeting his cold gaze with a sinking feeling in her stomach. 'I don't think there's any point in waiting out the six months. It will only make it harder for me. It's best if I leave now.'

A ripple of tension whipped over his face and his hands clenched into fists by his sides. 'Now? Are you crazy? You can't leave. We made an agreement.' There was a restricted quality to his voice. 'You'll lose everything if you leave now.'

Artie sighed. 'I can't be with you if you don't love me. It wouldn't be healthy for me. It would only reinforce the negative feelings I've had about myself in the past. That I'm not worthy, that I'm somehow the cause of everything bad that happens to me and those I care about. I need to leave that part of my life behind now. I need to embrace life as a fully awakened adult woman who knows what she wants and isn't afraid to ask for it.'

His hand scraped through his hair, leaving tracks in the thick black strands. He muttered a curse word in Italian, his mouth pulled so tight there were white tips at the corners. 'I can't stop you leaving but I should warn you there will be consequences. I'm not going to hand over a property with the potential of Castello Mireille just because you've pulled the plug on our agreement. I will keep it. I will develop it into a hotel and then I'll sell it.' His eyes flashed with green and brown sparks of anger. An anger so palpable it crackled in the air.

Artie ground her teeth, fighting to keep control of her own anger. 'Do what you need to do, Luca. I won't stand in your way. And I don't expect you to stand in mine.' She moved across to where she had left her phone. 'I'm going to call Rosa to come and get me.'

'Don't be ridiculous,' Luca said. 'It'll take her hours to get here.'

Artie faced him, phone in hand, eyebrows arched. 'Will you drive me?'

His top lip curled and his eyes turned to flint. 'You must be joking.'

Her chin came up. 'I'm not.'

He released a savage breath and muttered another curse. 'I'll organise a driver.' He took out his own phone and selected a number from his contacts.

Artie turned away as he told his employee to come and collect her for the journey back to Umbria. There was nothing in his tone to suggest he was shattered by her decision to leave him. He was angry, yes, but not devastated. Not as devastated as she was feeling. But how could he be? He didn't love her, so why would he feel anything but anger that she was pulling out of their agreement? His plans had been disrupted. His heart was unaffected.

Luca slipped the phone back in his pocket, his expression set in cold, emotionless lines. 'Done. Emilio will be here in five minutes.'

Artie moistened her parchment-dry lips again. Was this really happening? He was letting her go without a fight? It validated her decision to leave now, before she got even more invested in their relationship. But how much more invested could she be than what she was now? She loved him with her entire being and yet he felt nothing more for her than he would for a pet or a pot plant. He *cared* about her. That wasn't enough for her. It would never be enough. 'Thank you. I'd better go and pack a few things.' She turned for the door, waiting, hoping for him to call her back. She even slowed her steps, giving him plenty of time to do so. One step. Two steps. Three steps. Four...

'Artie.'

Her heart lifted like a helium balloon and she spun around. Had he changed his mind? Would he beg her to rethink her decision?

Oh, please, beg me to stay. Tell me you love me.

'Yes?'

His expression was mask-like but his throat rose and fell over a tight swallow. 'Keep safe.' His tone was gruff.

An ache pressed down on her chest, an avalanche of emotion that made it impossible for her to take a breath. Her eyes burned with unshed tears. She. Would. Not. Cry. Not now.

She would not make herself look any more gauche and desperate. She would take a dignified stance. She would take a leaf from his relationship playbook—she would be cool and calm and collected, detached. Their business deal was over and she would move on. End of story. 'You too. And thanks for…everything.' She pulled the heirloom engagement ring off her finger as well as the wedding band and held them out to him. 'You'd better take the rings back. The earrings and pendant are upstairs. I'll leave them on the dressing table.'

'Keep them.'

'But they're family heirlooms—'

'I said, keep them.' The words were bitten out through a paper-thin slit between his lips, a savage frown pleating his brow.

Artie put the rings on one of the side tables and then turned and walked out of the room, closing the door softly but firmly behind her.

CHAPTER TWELVE

As SOON AS the car carrying her away disappeared from sight Luca sucked in a breath that tore at his throat like wolf claws. What did she expect him to do? Run after her and beg her to stay? He had told her the terms from the outset. He had made it clear where his boundaries were.

But you shifted the boundaries. You slept with her.

He dragged a hand down his face, his gut clenching with self-disgust. Yes, he had shifted the boundaries and he should have known better. Artie was so young and inexperienced, and sleeping with him had made things so much worse. It had fuelled her romantic fantasies about him, fantasies he could never live up to. But he hadn't been able to help himself. He'd wanted her the moment he met her, maybe even before that.

She was light and he was darkness.

She was naïve and trusting and he was ruthless and cynical.

She was in touch with her emotions and he had none…well, none that he wanted to acknowledge. Emotions were not his currency. It was a language he didn't speak and nor did he want any fluency in it.

Luca picked up the engagement and wedding rings from the side table, curling his fingers around them so he didn't have to look at the mocking, accusing eyes of the diamonds. He rattled them in his hand like dice and tossed them back on the table, turning away with an expletive.

He was not going to go after her. He. Was. Not. He was *not* going after her. His old self would have run up the stairs even before she packed and got down on bended knee and begged her to stay.

But he was not that reckless teenage boy any more. He was able to regulate his reactions, to think logically and carefully about his actions. He was able to weigh the checks and balances and act accordingly…except when it came to making love with her. That had been reckless and ill-advised and yet he had done it anyway. Done it and enjoyed every pulse-racing second of it. Artie had got to him in a way no one else ever had.

He *felt* different.

Something inside him had changed and he wasn't sure he could dial it back. But he was damn well going to try.

Artie spent the first month back at Castello Mireille vainly waiting for the phone to ring. She longed to hear Luca's voice, she longed to feel his touch, to be in his arms again. She was suffering terrible withdrawal symptoms, missing the stroke and glide of his body within hers, the passionate press of his lips on her mouth, her breasts and her body. She reached for him in the middle of the night, her heart sinking when she found the other side of the bed cold and empty.

She realised with a sickening jolt that this was what her father had gone through after the accident. He had grieved both physically and emotionally for her mother. The loss of an intimate partner was felt on so many levels, little stabs and arrows every time you were reminded of the person, every time a memory was triggered by sight, sound, taste, touch or hearing.

Losing Luca was like a death. He was gone

from her life and she couldn't get him back, not unless she compromised herself in the process. And hadn't she compromised herself enough for the last decade? Denying herself any sort of life, any sort of enjoyment and happiness out of guilt?

She was no longer the girl in a psychological coma. She was awake to her potential, awake to what she wanted and no longer afraid to aim for it, even if it meant suffering heartbreak along the way. Luca was everything she wanted in a husband, but if he didn't love her, then how could she ever be happy settling for anything less than his whole heart?

Artie was working in the morning room on a christening gown for one of the villager's baby, waiting for Rosa to bring in morning tea. There was a certain sadness in working on babies' clothes when it was highly likely she would never have a baby now. How could she without Luca, the only man she wanted to have children with? The only man she could ever love? She placed another neat stitch in the christening gown, wondering what he was doing now. Working, no doubt. Visiting his grandfather. Taking a new lover to replace her... Her insides revolted at the thought of him making love to someone else. Artie forced herself to concentrate on her embroidery rather than torturing herself. The weeks since coming home, she had decided to pour her energy into her craft and had even set up a social media page and website. To take it from a hobby to a business. She had orders coming in so quickly she could barely keep up. But it gave her the distraction she needed to take her mind off Luca and their broken marriage.

Rosa came in carrying a tray with their refreshments. She set it on the table in front of Artie and then sat down beside her, taking a cup of tea for herself off the tray. 'I'm thinking about taking a little holiday. I know my timing isn't good, given the situation with you and Luca, but I thought it was time I saw a bit of the world outside these walls now you're a little more independent.'

Artie put the christening gown to one side, wrapping it in the white muslin cloth she used to protect it. 'Oh, Rosa, I feel bad you've been stuck here with me for so long. But you don't have to worry about me now. I've been to the village several times this week on my own and even had coffee at the café a couple of times. I can't say it's easy, but I do it and feel better for it.'

'I'm so glad you're able to do more.' Rosa sighed and continued, 'While you were staying with Luca, I realised I might have been holding you back. Don't get me wrong—I wanted to help you, but I think my reasons were not as altruistic as you think.'

Artie frowned. 'What do you mean?'

Rosa looked a little shamefaced. 'When I got my heart broken all those years ago, I locked myself away here working for your family. It was my way of avoiding being hurt again. But I worry that I might have inadvertently held you back by allowing you to become dependent on me.'

'You haven't done any such thing,' Artie said. 'I held myself back and now I'm moving forward. But I can't thank you enough for being there when I needed you.'

Rosa's expression was tender with concern. 'Have you heard from Luca?'

Artie sighed and shook her head. 'No. Nothing.'

'Have you called or texted him?'

Artie leaned forward to reach for a teacup. 'What would be the point? I told him how I feel and he didn't feel the same, so end of story. I have to move on with my life. Without him.'

Rosa toyed with the hem of her flowered dress in an abstracted manner. 'What will you do if or when he sells the *castello*?'

'I'll find somewhere else to live. I can't live in a place this big. It's not practical.' Artie's shoulders went down on a sigh. 'I'll always have wonderful memories of being here with Mama and Papa before the accident but it's well and truly time to move on. Someone else can live here and make their own memories.'

Rosa straightened the folds of her dress over her knees. 'The holiday I was telling you about...? I'm going with a...a friend.'

Artie's interest was piqued by the housekeeper's sheepish tone. She put the teacup back down on the table in front of her. 'Who is the friend?'

Twin spots of colour appeared in Rosa's cheeks. 'Remember I told you about the love of my life who got away? Well, Sergio and I met up while you were staying with Luca. We've been seeing each other now and again since. He's asked me to go away with him for a short holiday. I won't go if you need me here, though.'

Artie leaned over to give Rosa a hug. 'I'm

so happy for you.' She leaned back to look at her. 'I will always need you, Rosa, but as a friend, not as a babysitter.'

Rosa grimaced. 'You don't think I'm too old to be galivanting off with a man?'

Artie smiled. 'Not if you love him and he loves you.'

If only I should be so lucky.

Luca put off telling his grandfather about Artie leaving him for as long as he could because he didn't want to say the words out loud. *She left me.* But when Nonno was released from hospital and transferred into a cancer therapy unit, Luca had to explain why Artie wasn't with him. *She left me.* Those three words were like bullet wounds in his chest, raw, seeping, deep.

Nonno's distress at hearing Luca's news about his marriage was almost as bad as his own. 'But why? She's perfect for you, Luca. Why haven't you gone after her and brought her back?'

'Nonno, gone are the days when a man can carry a woman back to his cave,' Luca said. 'I can't force her to stay with me. She made the choice to leave.'

Nonno scowled. 'If you loved Artie like I

loved your grandmother, nothing would stop you from doing everything in your power to get her back. A man in love is a force to be reckoned with.'

The silence was telling.

Luca loosened the collar of his shirt and leaned forward to rest his forearms on his thighs. 'Enough about my dramas. Is there anything I can get you?'

Nonno shook his head and closed his eyes. 'No. I just need to sleep.'

Luca stood from the bedside and laid a gentle hand on his grandfather's weathered arm. 'I'll be in again tomorrow.'

He was on his way out of the hospital when his phone rang with his mother's ring tone and his chest seized with the all too familiar dread. But instead of letting his phone go to message service as he often did, this time he answered it. 'Mama.'

'Luca, how is Nonno? I tried calling him but he must have his phone off. His carer rang to tell me he had a fall a week or two ago. She also told me you're married. Is that true? Why didn't you invite me to your wedding?'

Guilt gnawed at his conscience. 'Nonno's doing okay. As to my marriage—it's a long story and I hate to tell you it hasn't got a happy ending.'

'Oh, Luca.' His mother's sigh only intensified the pain riddling his chest. 'What's happened to us that you didn't want me to be there on your special day?'

Luca cleared his suddenly blocked throat and stepped out of the way of visitors coming through the hospital entrance. He pinched the bridge of his nose, scrunching his eyes closed briefly. 'It's not you. It's me. It's always been me that's the problem.'

'You're too hard on yourself,' his mother said. 'You're so like your father it's uncanny.' She sighed again and went on, 'It's why I found it increasingly difficult to be around you as you grew into a man. I couldn't look at you without seeing him. It reminded me of my role in what happened.'

Luca frowned, his hand going back to his side. 'Your role? What are you talking about? I was the one who entered the surf that day. You weren't even at the beach.'

'No.' Her voice was ragged. 'I wasn't there. I went shopping instead of spending the day with my family as your father wanted. Do you know how much I regret that now? It's tortured me for years. What if I had gone along? I could've called for help instead of you trying to do it on your own. I can't bear to think of you running along that deserted beach, half drowned yourself, trying to find someone to help.' She began to sob. 'Whenever I've looked at you since, I've seen that traumatised, terrified young boy and felt how I let you and your papa and Angelo down.'

Luca blinked away stinging moisture from his eyes. He swallowed deeply against the boulder-sized lump in his throat. 'Mama, please don't cry. Please don't blame yourself. I'm sorry I haven't called you. I'm sorry I've let you suffer like this without being there for you. It was selfish of me.'

'You haven't got a selfish bone in your body,' his mother said. 'Your father was the same. Too generous for words, always hard-working, trying to make the world a better place. But tell me, what's going on with your marriage? It breaks my heart to think of you missing out on finding the love of your life. I'm so grateful I had those precious years with your father. They have sustained me through the long years since. I live off the memories.'

Luca gave a serrated sigh and pushed his hair back off his forehead. 'I'd rather not talk about it now, but next time I'm in New York do you want to catch up over dinner?'

'I would love that.' His mother's voice was thick with emotion. 'Give Nonno my best wishes.'

'*Sì,*' Luca said. 'I will.'

Luca tried not to think about Artie in the next couple of weeks and he mostly succeeded. Mostly. He blocked his memories of her smile, her touch and her kiss with a punishing regime of work that left him feeling ragged at the end of each day. One would think he would stumble into bed and fall instantly asleep out of sheer exhaustion, but no, that was when the real torture got going. The sense of emptiness could be staved off during the day but at night it taunted him with a vengeance. He tossed, he turned, he paced, he swore, he thumped the pillows and doggedly ignored the vacant side of the bed where Artie had once lain. He did his best to ignore the fragrance of her perfume that stubbornly lingered in the air at his villa as if to taunt him. He did his best to ignore the pain that sat low and heavy in his chest, dragging on his organs like a tow rope.

She left you.

But then more words joined in the mocking chorus.

You let her go.

He allowed them some traction occasionally, using them as a rationalisation exercise. Of course he'd let her go. It was the right thing to do. She wanted more than he could give, so it was only fair that he set her free.

But you're not free.

What was it with his conscience lately? Reminding him of things he didn't want reminding about. No, he didn't feel free and— even more worrying—he didn't *want* to feel free. He wanted to feel connected, bonded to Artie, because when he was with her, he felt like a fully functioning human being. He felt things he hadn't felt before. Things he didn't think he was capable of feeling. Things that were terrifying because they made him vulnerable in a way he had avoided feeling for most of his adult life.

He had shut down his emotional centre.

Bludgeoned it into a coma.

But since his conversation with his mother there were tiny flickers of life deep in his chest like the faint trace of a heartbeat on an electrocardiograph. A pulse of something he had thought long dead. A need he had denied for so long he had fooled himself he wasn't capable of feeling it.

The need to love and be loved.

Three more words popped into his head like a blinding flash of light.

You love her.

Luca let them sit for a moment, for once not rushing to block them or erase them or deny them.

You love her.

And then he tweaked them, substituting the 'you' for 'I'.

I love her.

Bringing himself inexorably closer to the truth, step by step.

I. Love. Her.

He embraced the truth of those words like someone sucking in oxygen after near strangulation.

I love her.

His chest ballooned with hope, positive energy zapping round his body.

I love her.

Luca snatched up his car keys and the wedding and engagement rings from the bedside table. He'd placed them there as a form of self-torture but now he couldn't wait to see them back on Artie's finger where they belonged. Nonno was right. Luca's love for Artie was a force to be reckoned with—nothing would stop him from bringing her home.

Artie heard a car roaring through the *castello* gates and her heart turned over. She peered through the window in the sitting room and saw Luca unfold his tall, athletic figure from his car. Her pulse picked up its pace, her heart slamming into her breastbone, her skin tingling all over.

He's here.

She walked as calmly as she could to open the front door, schooling her features into a mask of cool politeness. After all, there was no point setting her hopes too high— he hadn't made a single effort to contact her over the past month. 'Luca. What brings you here?' She was proud of her impersonal tone. It belied the tumult of emotions in her chest.

He stepped through the open doorway with brisk efficiency, closing it with a click behind him. 'You bring me here, *cara*. You and only you.' He stood there with his hands by his sides and his expression set in grave lines. He looked tired around the eyes and his face hadn't seen a razor in a couple of days. 'I need to talk to you.'

Artie took a step back, her arms folding across her chest, her chin lifting. 'To say what?'

He unpeeled her arms from around her body, taking her hands in his. 'I've been such a fool. It's taken me the best part of a month to realise what's been there all the time.' He squeezed her hands. 'I love you, *mia piccola*. I love you so damn much it hurts. I can't believe I let you go. Can you ever forgive me?' He blinked a couple of times and she was surprised to see moisture in his eyes. 'I made a terrible mistake in not telling you sooner. But I wasn't able to recognise it until it was too late.' He drew her closer, holding her hands against his chest. 'Tell me it's not too late. I love you and want to spend the rest of my life with you. Please say yes. Please say you'll come back to me. Please give me another chance to prove how much I adore you.'

Artie brought one of her hands up to his prickly jaw, stroking it lovingly. 'I never thought I'd hear you say those words to me. I had given up hope, especially over the last few weeks.'

He grimaced and hugged her tightly to his chest. 'Don't remind me what a stubborn fool I've been. I can never forgive myself for that. I was in such denial that I couldn't even bring up your name on my phone. I knew it would hurt too much, so I didn't do it. Classic avoidance behaviour.'

Artie eased back to smile up at him. 'You're here now, so that's the main thing. I've missed you so much. I felt only half alive without you.'

He framed her face with his hands. 'You're everything I could ever want in a life partner. You complete me, complement me and challenge me to be the best man I can be. I can barely find the words to describe how much you mean to me.'

'I love you too, more than I can say.'

Luca lowered his mouth to hers and happiness exploded through her being. He was here. He loved her. He wanted to spend the rest of his life with her. His kiss communicated it all, passionately, fervently, devotedly. Even the steady thud of his heartbeat under her hand seemed to say the same. *I love you. I love you. I love you.*

After a moment, Luca lifted his mouth off hers and took something out of his trouser pocket. He held the wedding and engagement rings between his fingers. 'I think it's time these were put back where they belong, don't you?'

'Yes, please.' Artie held out her hand for

him to slip them back on her ring finger. 'I'm never taking those rings off again.'

Luca smiled. 'I want you to meet my mother. Will you come to New York with me as soon as possible?'

Artie raised her eyebrows in delight. 'You've spoken to her?'

His face lit up with happiness. 'We had a chat about things and I realised how blinkered I'd been all these years, reading things into her behaviour that weren't accurate at all. You've taught me so much about myself, *cara*. I can never thank you enough for that. I hope you won't mind sharing my mother with me? I should warn you that she'll very likely shower you with love.'

'I won't mind sharing her at all. I can't wait to meet her.' Artie lifted her face for his kiss, her heart swelling with love. Her sad, closed-off life had somehow turned into a fairy tale. She was free from her self-imposed prison, and Luca, the man of her dreams, her Prince Charming, had claimed her as the love of his life.

Luca finally lifted his head and looked down at her with heart-stopping tenderness. 'Will you come away for a honeymoon with me after we visit my mother?'

'Just try and stop me.'

He stroked the curve of her cheek with his finger. 'I wasn't going to sell Castello Mireille.'

Artie smiled and gave him a fierce hug. 'I think on some level I knew that.' She eased back to look at him again. 'But I don't need it any more. What I need is you. It doesn't matter where I live as long as you're there with me.'

His eyes shimmered with emotion and her heart swelled with love to see how in touch with his feelings he was now. 'I've spent most of my life avoiding feeling like this—loving someone so much it hurts to think of ever losing them. I was in denial of my feelings from the moment I met you. You woke me to the needs I'd shut down inside myself. The need to love and be loved by an intimate partner. I can't believe how lucky I am to have found you.'

Artie pressed a soft kiss to his mouth. 'I'm lucky to have been found by *you*. If it hadn't been for you, I might still be locked away from all that life has to offer.'

Luca smiled, his eyes twinkling. 'I know it's early days, but maybe we can think about having those bambinos Nonno was talking about?'

She beamed with unfettered joy. 'Really? You want to have children?'

'Why not?' He kissed the tip of her nose. 'Building a family with you will be a wonderful experience. You'll be the best mother in the world.'

'I think you'll be an amazing father,' Artie said. 'I can't wait to hold our baby in my arms. I never thought I wanted to have a family until I met you. I didn't allow myself to think about it. But now it's like a dream come true.'

Luca gazed down at her with love shining in his eyes. 'Thank you for being you. Adorable, sweet, amazing you.'

Artie gave him a teasing smile. 'So, you don't think I'm too naïve and innocent for you now?'

'You're perfect for me.' He planted a smacking kiss on her lips. 'And as to remaining innocent, well, I'll soon take care of that.'

Artie laughed and flung her arms around his neck. 'Bring it on.'

* * * * *